Essex Sto

By Jeremy M. R. M.

Chapter 1

The train door opened at Stratford Station and two boisterous young men, wearing cheap suits and loud ties, came crashing on board. They sauntered along the aisle, dazzled by the bright lights, having been standing at the dark end of the platform, and spotted a row of three empty seats, opposite which a calm man in his thirties was sitting quietly. One of the young men slumped down beside the window, his large frame spilling over onto the next seat, his plump face glowing red.

"Oh Andy, mate, what a night that was!" he exclaimed loudly, his entire body exploding with laughter. "How many shots did we have? I completely lost count. Did you *see* those girls? Did you see them? Oh man they were ready for some action. Too bad we had to get the last train home."

"Yeah, Si. That Carol girl. She was coming onto me. Mate, she could really drink," replied his skinny, red-headed accomplice, who had silently slipped into the aisle seat. "You know I never thought life would be like this. Every night's a party. Every day is a buzz."

"Andy, will you give me a call in the morning? Just to make sure I get up."

"Won't your Mum wake you up?"

"No, she's gone to the beach hut at Clacton with Dad for a few days. Could you give me a call at five-thirty?" Both men were fully aware of the potential consequences of arriving late to their place of work including instant dismissal.

"All right, Si. Have you got your...you know...your little pick me up?" His thin, weaselly face erupted into a contorted grin.

"Yes, I've got enough for tomorrow. But I am getting a bit low..." Simon noticed the man sitting opposite for the first time. A handsome man with sandy shoulder-length hair, a trim beard, and clear blue eyes looking right back at him, who must surely have been listening to their conversation. "Shh!" he said forcefully to Andy and then he addressed the stranger, as if nothing unseemly had been said. "Hello, mate. How's it going? Had a good evening, have you? What've you been up to?"

The man smiled warmly and replied with a strong, deep voice. "I've been to see an old friend of mine. We had a nice evening, and I am fine thanks." He was casually dressed in jeans and a jumper. He held out his hand ready to shake Simon's podgy, sweaty paw. "My name is Jez. Pleased to meet you."

The youngster grabbed the outstretched hand clumsily. He often felt like a fish out of water and even the most rudimentary social customs sometimes caused him difficulty. "I'm Si and this is Andy, my very good mate."

Andy reached over to enact a firm, ceremonial Essex handshake. Despite inwardly feeling suspicious, he made confident eye-contact to create a warm impression. "Hello, mate. Where are you heading?"

"I'm going to Ingatestone – that's where I live," replied Jez. "What about you?"

"Same here. We're Ingatestone boys too! So, where abouts in Ingatestone do you actually live?"

"I live in a farm cottage up by the Hall. What about you two?"

"We both live in The Meads."

Andy was very proud of his rapid metamorphosis from country schoolboy into London banker.

"We're traders in the City – been doing that for about six months now. Long hours but we are doing great at it."

"Oh, I used to do something like that. I worked for one of the big Investment Banks for about ten years."

Simon was curious to know more. In contrast with his friend's bravado, he had some genuine concerns about how sustainable his current career choice might turn out to be. The trading hall sometimes seemed like a cut-throat, testosterone-fuelled Roman amphitheatre, which was a little outside his comfort zone to say the least. On top of that, the nightlife was relentless and there was almost an unwritten expectation for junior staff to indulge in dissolute behaviour with their bosses. Drugs were freely available and seemed to provide a certain degree of insulation from the huge financial risks that were a constant feature of the job.

"So, if you don't mind me asking, why did you stop?"

Jez sat back and paused. "I suppose you could say that I found God." The younger men turned to each other. Andy snorted with laughter. Simon smiled and put his finger to his lips to signal that they should perhaps respectfully listen to what the older man was about to say. Jez continued.

"You see, I was caught up in a life of almost endless drinking. I was desperately trying to stay on top of it, but it got to a point where I had to drink

3

even to be able to do the simplest things. Even to tie my shoelaces in the morning!

"I did a good job of hiding it for years. As you might imagine, there were plenty of other people at the office who liked to over-indulge in alcohol or drugs. But in the end, it just became obvious that I was falling apart. I had got caught up in some dodgy business, *really* bad stuff, and so one day I just quit the job, walked out of the office, and never went back.

"Then it really started to hit me. I had nothing: no job, no home, no family and ... no hope. There were some issues from my past, nagging away at me, that I needed to face up to. So, I decided to make a new start. I quit drinking, and I got into recovery."

"Wow," interrupted Andy. "You must have been *really* desperate to do that!"

"I was. And then I met my friend, John, the one I was with tonight. He helped me like a father. He had nearly drunk himself to death – it damaged his heart. But he pulled through. Now he spends most of his time helping people with drink problems.

"John understood me like nobody else ever had before, and I trusted him and told him everything about me. 'I can't help you, Jez,' he told me, 'but I know a man who can. You just need to follow him and learn how to love other people and you will be fine.' So, I started along a different path.

"It hasn't been easy but now my life is fulfilling and worthwhile, as long as I help other people. If they want me to, that is."

Both the younger men had both been surprisingly engaged by Jez's story and listening to it seem to have jolted them into becoming relatively sober. Simon was already starting to feel strangely hooked

4

by this man's approach to life. He had never heard anybody speak like this before. Yes, he had been to church and had attended religious education classes at school. But none of it had seemed particularly real to him – more like fairy tales. Suddenly here was a man, full of charm and vitality, who appeared to have something more concrete and compelling to say about spiritual matters and how he had put them into practice. Was this what he'd been missing?

Andy was also moved by what he had heard, albeit to a lesser extent than his friend. This staggered him somewhat as he was both an atheist and vehemently anti-religion, in common with most his family. His Dad always said that if you have a problem then it's up to you to 'pull yourself together and sort yourself out'. And this mantra of self-sufficiency had stood Andy in good stead most of the time, so far. He tended to regard people who professed to depend on supernatural power as being weak and lacking self-belief. He could argue against the existence of God with the best of them. 'If there is a God,' he would say, 'why does he allow so many bad things to happen in the World?' Plus, the news was always full of priests abusing children.

And yet faced with the charismatic presence of this man sitting opposite him, calmly explaining how he had turned his life around, through his faith, he felt no desire to challenge what he was saying. Something primitive inside him was yearning for a deeper level of existence and here was a tantalising glimpse of a life beyond the bounds of his current world of High Finance. However, he was enjoying something of a honeymoon period in this exciting adult arena. It was going to take a lot to shake him out of that.

The conversation flowed as the train rattled along the track into rural Essex. A nice rapport was developing between the three men. There were other travellers in their midst, but they were either pre-occupied with their personal devices or snoozing and none of them was paying any attention to what was being said.

"So I have told you a little bit about my life," said Jez. "I see that we are about to arrive at our stop, but if you would like to continue our conversation for a while you are very welcome to come along to my cottage for a cup of tea. I would love to get to know you better."

"Oh, I don't know," replied Andy. "It's late and we gotta get up early."

"Come on, mate!" insisted his friend, "It's Friday tomorrow – we don't have to stay too long."

So, the three men got out of the train together, into the moonless April night, quietly walked through the car park, and then began to stroll up the narrow lane towards Jez's cottage.

Chapter 2

Simon and Andy had not been to this part of the village for a few years although it had been one of their favourite boyhood playgrounds. Here had been endless vistas of farmyards and fields, interspersed with woodlands. Here it had been a delightful experience to while away summer days, far from home and parents, learning about themselves and their peers, beginning to see girls in a different way.

On this quiet night they felt more alert and attuned to nature than usual, despite the alcohol they had consumed earlier. They were aware of the rustling of small animals in the hedgerows and the hooting of an owl in the trees.

* * *

Jez pointed to a narrow track along the side of the farmhouse. "My cottage is down this path," he said, leading the way, and using his phone as a torch. "Be careful where you tread. There are a few holes to watch out for." Soon they arrived at a decrepit outbuilding. Jez pulled the key from his pocket. Pushing the heavy door open, he turned on the light. The accommodation was basic. It was essentially a small barn with some rudimentary furniture and cooking equipment. There was a coarsely home-built bed in a corner and a door which presumably led to the bathroom facilities. A washing line was suspended between two rafters with clothes hanging from it. There was also an electric heater which seemed barely adequate for the size of the building.

"I'll put the kettle on; you guys take a seat." Simon and Andy made themselves comfortable on the old, worn sofa. Jez made neither apology nor explanation for the elementary nature of his home. And this was not necessary as Simon and Andy felt perfectly relaxed in this environment.

"So, what kind of work do you do, Jez?" inquired Simon. "If you don't mind me asking?"

"Oh, I help out here on the farm," he replied. "I'm good with my hands. I can repair the farm machinery. And I like to do woodwork. It's a never-ending job to keep all the barns shipshape. And I look after the fences and pathways around the site."

"A bit of a change from what you were doing in the City, then?"

"Oh yes. And I prefer this line of work."

"But you must have been getting paid a hell of a lot more back then?" interjected Andy.

"I was. But it wasn't right for me. Money isn't everything, you know. Rules were being broken and people's lives were being damaged. I ended up feeling shallow. Rotten to the core!"

"So you gave it all up to come and live here?"

"Yeah. Nowadays I prefer to earn my money legally, honestly and without harming others. I don't have much but I'm much happier.

"There's an old saying that love of money is the root of all evil. It's sad to see how true this still is today. Some people are so busy trying to get ahead, or stay ahead, that they neglect the really important things in life. Like friendship, romantic love or parenthood. They are always too busy making money to actually live!

"And, what's more, for every winner in the game of money there are many losers."

"But that's part of the fun," remarked Andy. "It's all a game, like gambling. And as long as you don't take it too seriously, what's wrong with that?"

"Well I believe that the world was created for us all to enjoy equally. If I take more than my share, then it follows that somebody else is going to miss out. I find that I am happier if I just have what I need.

"I try to live my life by three basic rules: firstly, to help other people, secondly to respect the planet, and thirdly to do what I think God wants me to do. You'll have noticed that I talk about God quite a lot. I know that's not for everyone."

"Yeah – no offence, but I don't really believe in any of that stuff."

"No offence taken. It's up to you what you believe in. But I do think it's important to believe in *something*. Something to protect you and to guide you to make the right choices.

"You don't *have to* believe in God to live like me. As long as you try to do the next right thing, you can substitute whatever works for you."

Simon and Andy paused to reflect on what they just heard. They were not accustomed to discussing deep and personal matters openly like this.

Simon began to question his career choice again. Sometimes it seemed that it was *all* about 'love of money' and gambling – at least that's what he picked up from conversations with his colleagues. Of course, there were arguments to be made about banking being essential to progress and global economic development. But there was a big question developing in his mind about *how* this was being done. What did Jez mean about rules being broken and people being damaged? He couldn't explain it yet, but something wasn't sitting right with him.

Andy had been taking on board Jez's observations and evaluating them against his own philosophy of self-reliance. So far, he had found riding the rollercoaster of financial risk, and coming out on top, more often than not, to be highly exhilarating. It all came down to natural selection – life is just a game where there are bound to be winners and losers.

The kettle boiled, and Jez made a pot of tea which he brought over to the small table in front of the sofa. As he poured it out into mugs, he continued to elucidate his recipe for living.

"There is a lot of spiritual sickness in this world which needs to be healed. The rules that people follow are not always the right ones. This can lead them to unhappiness and despair. Everybody's life is precious.

"Nothing upsets me more that harm being done to a little, innocent child. That can wreck their life and deprive them of the happiness and fulfilment that they were meant to enjoy." Jez seemed to become emotional, as though what he had just said had resonated with something from his own past. He hesitated a while to compose himself and then he resumed. "And when I say 'child', I really mean all of us, for we are all God's children."

This was all a bit too much for Andy. It was time to inject a bit of pragmatism into the conversation and for Jez to get off his cloud. "I can see where you're coming from, Jez. You're making some good points, there. But's there's absolutely nothing we can do about it. The world is what it is. Shit happens. And you've just got to make the most of it, ride your luck, and sort out your own problems."

Jez sensed that he had struck a raw nerve here in the soft underbelly of Andy's doctrine. "Are you sure about that, Andy? What if you *could* make a difference? What if you could make some changes in your life and lead by example to show other people that there could be a better way?"

"Well, I don't know. Right now, we are making good money and everything's pretty exciting. Why would we want to change anything now just when life is really starting for us?"

To Andy's surprise, Simon took an opposing stance. "I'm not sure whether I'm really enjoying it all that much, actually, mate. I hate having to get up so early every day and go out drinking every single night. I have to take pills just to get out of bed in the morning. I'm constantly scared shitless that I'm really going to screw up and lose millions of pounds. It feels like I'm flying by the seat of my pants all the time. I don't really have a bloody clue what I'm doing. But I don't know what else I could do if I want to get on. I can't see what other job I could do where I could ever get the money I need to get on the housing ladder."

Andy looked down at the floor. He felt conflicted. He wanted to earn good money but, until Simon had mentioned his unrest, he had been putting his own to the back of his mind.

"Listen," said Jez, breaking the silence that had struck, "Do you boys like to go out clubbing?"

"Well, yes, of course we do," answered Simon, both surprised and curious to know where this might be leading.

"Okay then. Tomorrow you can come out clubbing with me in Chelmsford. But it will be clubbing with a difference. We are going out on a kind of rescue mission to find some poor souls that could maybe do with some help. What do you say?"

Andy and Simon looked at each other and pulled comically confused faces.

"What do you mean exactly, Jez? Are you expecting us to stand in front of all our mates with tambourines dressed up like the Salvation Army, or something?" asked Andy cheekily.

Jez laughed. "No. Of course not. It's mainly going to be like a normal Friday night out clubbing, but we will just be ready to help anybody that needs it. Perhaps you had both better drink up and head home now, as you've got to go to work in the morning. Come over and meet me here tomorrow evening around eight and we'll head out to town together?"

Chapter 3

Having spent much of their day replaying the events of the previous one in their minds, Simon and Andy were now strolling back towards Jez's simple dwelling with feelings of curiosity and excitement. After work they had returned home and had dressed up in their customary weekend clubbing attire: chinos, casual shirts, dark blazers and deck shoes. This had had the unfortunate effect of emphasizing certain imperfections of their respective physiques, with Simon's ample belly pushing against his shirt buttons and squeezing out over his trouser belt and Andy's bony ribcage and spindly legs barely filling his clothes at all.

It was not unusual on a Friday for the world's markets to function on lower levels of adrenalin than average and work had passed quite uneventfully today. Both men had found themselves carefully watching their colleagues and wondering, perhaps for the first time, whether these people were suitable role models, with their grey faces and their hands which trembled as they suckled on cup after cup of overly strong coffee.

There was a spit of rain in the cold air as they reached the path to Jez's cottage. On hesitantly arriving at the door, both men felt a surge of anxiety. Simon took a deep breath and looked across at Andy for reassurance before knocking directly on the wooden door with his knuckle.

The door opened and they were met by Jez's gently smiling face together with his striking turquoise-hued eyes. "Good evening, guys!" he said. "Come on in. It's great to see you!" They entered the small building, the warmth of their host's welcome quickly putting them at their ease. He was dressed smartly in a blue suit and open-necked shirt, with immaculately polished brown leather shoes. Andy was relieved to see that he wouldn't look out of place in a nightclub environment, having half expected him to have turned up wearing sandals and a kaftan.

"Simon, Andy, take a seat and I'll make you a cuppa. Shall we have something to eat before we go out? I've got some nice bread and cheese here," said Jez.

"I wouldn't say no," replied Simon, who had already spotted a tempting basket of crusty rolls together with a large slab of Cheddar on the kitchen table.

"Yeah, me too please, mate," said Andy.

Usually, Simon and Andy were in the habit of partaking of a substantial 'pre-drink drink', on a clubbing night. This was in order to lower their inhibitions without needing to pay inflated nightclub alcohol rates. But on this occasion the urge had not hit them and, anyway, it would have seemed disrespectful to ask their host for a drink, who yesterday had opened up about his past struggles with alcohol.

"Let's stay here for a couple of hours and have a chat and then we'll head over to Chelmsford around eleven. I'll take us in the farm's Land Rover," said Jez.

Time passed pleasantly and easily as the three men talked more about their general philosophies of life.

* * *

The vehicle was unorthodox for a night out, but Simon and Andy enjoyed the ride, and having parked by the ice rink, they all headed into the heart of town along the riverside path. As they approached the Fox and Hounds pub, a hideous modern structure of steel and glass, they became aware of a shuffling figure in the shadows and a sense of danger in the air.

Suddenly a dishevelled young man stepped out in front of them, with an open cider bottle in his hand. He caught Simon's eye watching him and said, "What are you looking at?"

"Oh nothing, mate, honestly," replied Simon, feigning a nervous grin.

"What are you fucking smiling at? You fucking arsehole!" said the stranger menacingly.

Simon felt panicky. He had been in a few situations like this before and he was not very good at handling them. On previous occasions, he had been lucky in that streetwise friends had been around to rescue him.

The drunken man continued, "I suppose you think you're better than me, don't you? Look at you in your poncey suit."

"I think that you need to calm down, mate!" replied Simon, putting his hands up to try to placate the angry man.

"Don't you 'mate' me. I ain't your fucking mate!" raged the man.

Andy thought he had better say something. "Just leave it out, *mate*," he interjected, antagonising the drunken man further. He was also quite inept at dealing with confrontation, though he was courageous and eager to protect his friend.

The enraged man smashed the bottle down on the railings along the riverbank and then charged towards Simon and Andy with the jagged edge raised threateningly towards them.

Jez had been carefully assessing the situation up until this point. Now he fearlessly stepped in front of Simon and Andy and firmly grabbed the drunken man's wrist that was holding the broken bottle with one hand, keeping his other hand free to protect against any other form of violence.

To Simon and Andy's surprise, Jez showed no sign of anger. In fact, he smiled warmly and disarmed the man with kindness. "Don't be afraid, my friend," he said to him. "We don't mean you any harm."

The underlying terror behind this man's angry eyes was clear to see. "What's your name, friend?" asked Jez.

"I'm Kieran," he muttered, surely baffled by the turn the confrontation had taken.

"I'm Jez and these are my friends, Simon and Andy. Now put down the bottle, Kieran." He gently brought down the man's hand and let go. The man put the broken bottle down on the ground. "Thank you, Kieran. That's better."

"Now, I want you to know something, Kieran. God loves you. He loves you very much." The fear and anger had melted away from the disturbed man's face. He smiled and shuffled off into the night.

"That was amazing, man!" exclaimed a very relieved Simon to Jez.

Just then, they were startled by a shrill, ear-splitting sound coming from around their ankles.

They looked down to see a swarm of about fifty black rats swirling and shrieking in a panic. A particularly large rat broke away from the pack, heading over towards the river and proceeded to disappear into the cold water, soon to be followed by all the others, splashing in behind.

There is an old adage that you are never more than six feet away from a rat, although most of us rarely see one. On this occasion, an entire colony of these unloved animals seemed to have become agitated by the fear and anger emanating from the disturbed man.

"What the…?" exclaimed Andy incredulously.

"Come on!" implored Jez. "It's all over now. Let's clean up the broken glass and head over to Stratton's Bar to have some fun!"

Soon the three of them arrived at the nightclub and engaged in some friendly chit-chat with the bouncers. Once inside, Jez asked, "What are you drinking, boys? It's my round!"

"Are you sure, mate?" replied Andy.

"Yes, of course. Now what are you both having?"

"All right, then. I'll have a JD and Coke."

"Me too," chimed in Simon eagerly.

So, he bought them both a Jack Daniels and Coke and a tonic water for himself.

The general atmosphere in the bar was cordial and, as much as the loud music would allow, they engaged in conversation with the other clients. Simon and Andy were regulars at this bar. They had a fairly large group of acquaintances there this evening, most of whom they had known since schooldays. They felt rather proud to introduce their new friend to this social group and couldn't wait to tell them about how he had pacified the bottle-wielding drunk. Their companions were, for the most part, delighted to meet this charming and confident older figure and somewhat intrigued as to how Simon and Andy had managed to befriend him.

Soon everybody was on the dance floor, including Jez. He danced with many of the women, but not in a flirtatious manner. After all, they were barely out of their teens, and his main mission tonight was to find people that needed his help.

The time spent in the club was enjoyable and passed without any major events. When it was time to leave, the three men affectionately bade farewell to the group. Before long Jez, Simon and Andy were striding back happily along the riverside path to the carpark. Once again, they happened upon some trouble.

A group of three middle-aged men was taunting a somewhat bedraggled woman, squatting on the floor with her hands over ears. She looked somehow less than human, more like a heap of bones and old clothes.

"Come on, Maggie, we know what you like! I'll come and sort you out," said a portly, balding figure, dripping with sweat. He, and his two accomplices, laughed loudly and coarsely. Then they began to prod the woman with their shoes, and chanting her name, menacingly, "Maggie! Maggie! Maggie!"

Jez walked up to the melee, and bravely pushed the men aside. "Stop that, please," he said. They looked at him with astonishment.

"Now tell me, gentlemen, how would you like it if somebody was treating your sister as you are treating this lady?" he asked. "You wouldn't like it at all, would you? Well, this lady is my sister and I don't like it! So, I would like you to leave now."

The bullies glanced at each other, as though slightly embarrassed and ashamed. They slipped off into a side road. Meanwhile, the relieved woman raised her head to meet Jez's gaze. Now, on closer inspection, he could see that, despite being somewhat weather beaten and wearing very tatty clothes. she was an attractive, dark-skinned woman of around twenty-five, with astonishing bright eyes.

"Hello. I'm Jez. These are my friends, Simon and Andy. So is Maggie your real name?"

"Yes, it is, Sir. Short for Margaret," she replied respectfully. "Thank you for helping me."

"I hope you won't mind me asking, Maggie, but do you have somewhere to stay tonight?"

"No, I've been living on the streets for a while," she replied but, fearing she might have revealed more than she should have, she continued, "Don't worry. You get used to it; you know."

"I live in a cottage on a farm near here. It's nothing special but it's warm and dry. If you like, you can come and stay with me for a while. Until you find somewhere better to live. Don't worry – you can trust me. I only want to make sure you are safe."

Maggie pondered for a moment. This was a strange and unexpected offer – experience told her that there had to be a catch! She had been used and hurt by many men many times before. This guy seemed respectable. Plus, he was good looking! He didn't seem like the type who needed to take a street girl home to get his sexual fix.

She was used to danger and this didn't seem any more dangerous than staying where she was. So yes, she was interested. "Are you sure you want to help me?" she asked.

Jez tried to reassure her. "Of course, I want to. I promise that you can trust us... So, will you come?"

"All right then," she replied a little half-heartedly.

"Do you have some belongings you need to collect first, Maggie? If you show us where, we'll take them with us."

Maggie led them to the shop front where she had been sleeping. Her possessions consisted only of a sleeping bag and several plastic bags containing clothes, one of which doubled up as an ad hoc pillow. There was also evidence nearby of drug misuse — remnants of tin foil and matches. Maggie realised that Jez had spotted these and gasped with embarrassment. To her relief, Jez simply gave her a reassuring glance, and nothing was said.

The three men carried Maggie's bags back to the Land Rover and then they headed back on the road to Ingatestone with their extra passenger.

Chapter 4

The four friends were sitting contently on makeshift chairs of upside-down crates around the small kitchen table. The oldest among them sat quietly observing the other three conversing excitedly and looking for answers. He felt a sense of avuncular pride in how their curious minds were starting to blossom.

A week had passed since the eventful night in Chelmsford when Simon, Andy and Jez had met Maggie and Jez had offered her refuge in his cottage. There was evidence that she had settled in well. A separate bedroom for her had been created by partitioning off a space using a blanket and a couple of wooden slats. A fold-up bed had also appeared next to the sofa for Jez to sleep in. There were several bowls of wild flowers in the room, too: one of which was prominently placed in the centre of the table at which she now sat, with her new friends, eating a delicious meal of fresh vegetable broth and home-baked bread. The contents of the plastic bags she had brought with her had been magically transformed into a small and neat pile of fresh smelling women's clothes.

She had, in fact, spent her first two days in Ingatestone mainly in bed, being cared for by Jez, and going cold turkey from her heroin habit. The level of discomfort she had experienced had been far less severe that with previous withdrawals. There had been some sweating, shaking and abdominal pains. But her anxiety had been largely offset by a new sense of hope, together with Jez's kindness to her.

Simon and Andy had just finished another week at work. It had been a different experience from before. In Simon's case it had felt as though his attitudes were changing. He was no longer in awe of the show-offs at the office and he felt less worried about his lack of suitability for the position he currently held. A vague, yet more attractive, Plan B seemed to have been emerging since he had met Jez. He felt less concerned with personal material progress and more interested in other people. He had not felt the need to replenish his supply of recreational drugs this week. The ritualistic downing of 'shots' with colleagues had merely seemed to him like going through the motions. It would have been much better to have spent that time here, with his real friends!

Andy was still enjoying the office work, the buzz of excitement regarding placing risky trades, and participating in the office banter with those around him. Something was different, however. He had started to become attuned to the human side of his colleagues. He was not usually a very empathetic person, but he had found himself speculating about hidden motives of certain toxic individuals that he was observing. The angry and unforgiving team manager, her apologetic and emasculated deputy, and the brash and arrogant senior trader.

As soon as the meal was finished, Andy spoke. "Why don't you play some of your music, Si? He's very good at making music tracks. I asked him to bring his iPad. That'd be all right, wouldn't it, Jez?"

"Yes, of course it would. What kind of music do you make, Simon?" asked Jez.

"Well it's just a hobby, nothing special. But what I do is to sample some music from a song that I like. Then I add some effects, some drumbeats, maybe other instruments and turn it into something new," replied Simon.

"And he raps!" interjected Andy excitedly.

"Well, I guess it's a kind of rap. I mean, I like to make up some new words and add them over the top."

"That sounds great. I'd love to hear some," enthused Jez.

Simon felt his heart racing. He worried that Jez, in particular, and Maggie too might find his creative efforts somewhat laughable. Fear of ridicule had been a constant feature of his life as far back as he could remember. There had been a lot of teasing about his weight, both at home and at school. Yes, he had learned to laugh along with it and shrug it off, but sometimes there is only a fine line between teasing and bullying. He remembered being asked to stand up and sing in front of his class when he was at primary school when he had felt so nervous that he hadn't been able to sing at all and had just started to cry.

Anyway, best just get it over with! There was no way to backtrack now. "This track is called 'Job in the City'," he said. Andy was smiling with anticipation that this would be well received.

So, Simon started to play the track from his IPad. It began with a catchy syncopated drumbeat and then several fugue-like musical layers were introduced one-by-one until the main hook started. This was a sampled saxophone solo from the song 'Careless Whisper' by George Michael.

Once that was over, he started to rap. The words were naïve and unsophisticated, but they were recited in a catchy rhythmic counterpoint to the underlying drumbeat.

> *I got a job in the City,*
> *Where the girls are so pretty,*
> *It's Simon and Andy,*
> *We're getting very handy.*

Andy's voice could also be heard accompanying Simon's on certain keywords, for the purpose of emphasis.

"So... what do you think?" asked Andy in expectation, when it was over.

"I love it!" said Jez. "The rhythm is great and it's really creative." Simon's heart rose on hearing this. Then Jez looked across to Maggie. "What do you think?"

"I like it too," she replied politely. Perhaps it was a bit corny but there were some interesting ideas.

"Do you like to sing or play any instruments, Maggie?" asked Jez.

"Well, I did use to sing in Church when I was younger. But it all stopped when I had to leave home," she replied.

"Oh, some Church songs are beautiful. There is one that I really like with lots of Hallelujahs in it." He laughed. "Goes a bit like this: 'Hallelujah, Hallelu, Hallelujah'. Do you know that song, Maggie?"

"Yes, yes, I do. I love that song! It's called 'Seek Ye First the Kingdom of God'."

"I'd love to hear you sing it, Maggie. Would you sing it to us?" asked Jez.

Maggie blushed and felt her nerves jangling. She noticed that Simon and Andy were both looking at her with interest. So, she closed her eyes, composed herself and sang the words of the song.

> *Seek ye first the Kingdom of God*
> *And His righteousness*
> *And all these things shall be added unto you*
> *Hallelujah, Hallelujah.*

Her voice was clear and sweet but was also tinged with pain. As she sang, some long-buried emotions awoke within her, both happy and sad, causing her voice to crack in a few places.

After she had finished, the three men all felt moved and gave her a spontaneous round of applause. They had genuinely appreciated hearing her voice. It had been an awfully long time since she had felt anything like this.

"We certainly have a lot of talent here tonight," said Jez. "Why don't we clear the table and then make some music together. May we use your iPad, Simon?"

"Yes, sure," replied Simon.

Jez continued. "You know, I've been wondering about new ways to reach people who need help. We could make a music video to get across what we stand for and then post it on YouTube to try to find people that way. Are you guys up for doing that?"

"Do you mean a video about God and stuff like that?" retorted Andy with a distinctly horrified look. "To tell the truth, I'd be a bit embarrassed. What if people from work saw it? Or people we were at school with?"

"I don't want to pressurise any of you into doing anything you're not comfortable with. And I certainly wouldn't want you to say anything that you don't believe in yourself. We are all at different points in our spiritual journeys but perhaps we can find something to say that we all agree on. And it might just help somebody, you never know."

Simon made a decision. "I'll do it," he said. "People have been taking the mickey out of me all my life. When it comes down to it, I'm a bit of a laughing stock anyway. What have I got to lose?"

"I'll do it too," said Maggie. "Last week I was about as low as I could get – a drugged-up, homeless, street girl. Anything's got to be better than that. I'm on my way back up now."

"That's great, you two!" said Jez. "Andy, are you sure we can't twist your arm? Why don't you just see how it goes? And if you want to join in the rapping with Simon later feel free to do so. I promise we won't post anything to social media unless you are all completely happy with it. No pressure at all."

"All right," agreed Andy.

So, the project began. First Simon downloaded an instrumental version of the song to sample. Then using the music-creation software on his Pad, he laid down a drumbeat and a synthesized bass guitar riff. He had an extremely good ear for music. This had been remarked upon by a music teacher during his school days, but he had never really been encouraged to exploit it.

Then he recorded and filmed Maggie singing the chorus.

> *Hallelujah, Hallelujah,*
> *Hallelujah, Hallelujah, Hallelujah.*

He realised he would also have to utilise some video editing software to assemble the final offering to be published on YouTube.

"Maggie, when you were in the church choir, did you ever use to sing descants over the choruses?" asked Jez.

"I don't think I know what that is," she replied.

"It's a kind of high harmony that sits above the melody," he explained. And, to demonstrate, he sang a little of the chorus himself transposed into a slightly comic high-pitched falsetto. Simon and Andy groaned! But Jez was determined. "Do you think you could have a go at doing that?"

"I'll have a go, if you like."

Simon played the tracks that had been created so far: the drums, the bass, the sampled instrumental, and Maggie's rendition of the chorus. "Now sing something above that," said Jez, "Just let go and give it all you've got!"

Simon restarted the tracks and Maggie sang a soaring improvised vocal line above it that seemed to add an extra dimension of spiritual beauty to the song.

The next stage was for Simon to create the rap track. He had thought up a few rhyming couplets about 'Si and Andy' coming back from the City, how they had met Jez, their adventures in Chelmsford with the drunk, the rats and the homeless girl who was so pretty. (For Maggie was indeed extremely pretty!) He managed to cajole Andy into joining in by proposing some particularly crass or corny lyrics which he then felt duty-bound to help craft into something that sounded cooler.

Finally, Jez added his contribution which he spoke over a looped section in the music.

We walk through this world as sisters and brothers
Loving God and loving one another.

Simon completed the video edits and the four friends watched the resulting film together. The format was simple. It started with view of then all sitting around the table and talking as the catchy drum and bass music started. Next there were close-ups of Simon and Andy facing the camera and rapping. This led to a softened shot of the beautiful Maggie singing the chorus after which the spotlight moved to Jez, speaking out clearly and confidently.

"Okay, are we ready to launch this?" asked Simon. Everyone nodded their heads in agreement.

"It's actually pretty damned good!" admitted Andy.

Jez smiled back at him with delight. "I'm glad you're happy with it, Andy... Now since we are all agreed on this, I guess we should go ahead and create a channel on YouTube and decide on a name for our video. What do people think?"

"How about 'New Life'?" suggested Maggie.

"For the channel or the video?" asked Andy.

"Hmmm, for both!" she replied.

Five minutes later, it was done. Then, with some trepidation, Andy and Simon posted links on their assorted social-media channels.

"What have we done?" asked Andy worriedly, looking at Simon. He had put his name to, and publicised, a video which contained some distinctly religious, or at least quasi-religious, messages. "We're going to get rinsed for this!"

"It's not too late to change your mind, Andy," Jez reassured him. "But I think you guys have created something really great. Let's just see how it goes."

The four sat in silence for around ten minutes, mulling over their evening's work. Then, suddenly, Simon's iPhone chimed. He stared at the screen in disbelief for a while and then looked up.

"We just got our first 'like'!" he said.

Chapter 5

Another week passed and Maggie and Jez had been working together on the farm. It was useful to Jez to have another pair of hands, plus it was genuinely nice to have her company. So far, they had been repairing fences that had been damaged by winter gales, and creosoting the barns.

Maggie had particularly enjoyed rediscovering her singing voice and creating the video with the others. The 'New Life' YouTube channel was already getting a lot of attention and they had been contacted by people from around the world, keen to know more about them.

Now, as she stood with a paintbrush in her hand, wearing a pair of Jez's creosote-splattered dungarees, she began to wonder about this strange character who stood at her side, also painting the barn. Did he have a girlfriend? What were his intentions towards her? He was a good-looking man who seemed to treat her more like a family member than a potential partner.

Maggie had had a rough ride with men so far. She had left home at fifteen to escape the unwanted attentions of her stepfather and had been through a number of abusive relationships. Later she had resorted to prostitution to feed her drug habit, most recently in Chelmsford where she had become homeless. There had certainly been a lot of hairy experiences along the way, so it was refreshing to meet a man who genuinely seemed to be interested in her just for the person that she was.

She had told Jez all about her past and the mistakes she had made. Because he had been open with her, it had been surprisingly easy to pour out her darkest and most dreadful secrets to him. Jez helped her to see that most of these related to wrongs that had been done to her and that she was the victim and not the one to blame. Best just to accept them as being in the past and move on. There were a few mistakes, however, for which she needed to take responsibility and look for opportunities to put them right. She had caused distress to her mother by running away from home, she had stolen to pay for drugs, and she had abused her body in many ways. But he reassured her that everybody made mistakes, and that she would be forgiven for hers.

This had been a cathartic experience which made her feel wonderful inside. She felt an urge to share this feeling with other people and began to understand why Jez said repeatedly that it was so important to help others. Of course, there was a long road ahead to recovery – she was still carrying many scars from her past.

Once they had finished painting the barn, it was time to take the daily tour of the grounds in the Land Rover. The grounds were easily accessible by road and it was important to check that nothing untoward had happened since the previous inspection. As they approached the Stock Lane entrance, Jez noticed something and pointed ahead. "I wonder what that is. It looks worrying!" he said anxiously. Maggie saw that there was smoke rising in front of them.

They pulled up at the gate. Jez was silent. He jumped out of the Land Rover without looking at Maggie. and ran towards the drainage ditch. She had never seen him so unsettled before. He dropped to his knees in front of the ditch, raised his arms to the sky, and shouted angrily, "This is the beautiful Earth that has been given to us to enjoy and they just want to destroy it!"

Maggie also got out of the vehicle and quickly walked over to where Jez was kneeling. Then she saw what Jez was so upset about. Several blue barrels of the kind used to transport industrial chemicals had been dumped in the ditch. The barrels were cracked, and some unpleasant smelling liquid was oozing out into the soil and smoking. Alongside the barrels there was a heap of broken masonry and rusty metal objects. It was a real mess that would take a lot of effort to remove and to safely dispose of.

After a while, Jez turned his head to Maggie, still obviously perturbed. She put her hand on his shoulder and smiled at him. He relaxed. "I am sorry about that. You know how important looking after the Earth is to me. Don't worry, though. I can get this mess sorted out. I will need to get some help and we can do that tomorrow. For now, we can just cover it up with the polyurethane sheet that I keep in the back of the Land Rover."

Maggie nodded in agreement. "It's terrible that people do things like that." She sat, chin in hand, wondering what she might do to cheer Jez up. Then she had an idea. "Hey! Why don't we make another video about looking after the planet with Simon and Andy?"

* * *

Simon and Andy were standing up at the bar in Stratford, waiting for a tray full of shots to be served, which they had ordered for themselves and their older colleagues, Steve and Maxie.

"I'm getting some dodgy vibes off the guys tonight, Si," remarked Andy. "Something doesn't feel right. They seem to be really annoyed with us."

"Let's just go with the flow," Simon replied, gesticulating towards the drinks. "Hopefully, these will cheer them up."

When the drinks had all been served, Simon carried the tray over to the pedestal where their companions were standing and silently watching him.

"Down the 'atch!" said Maxie, a small wiry man in his forties with grey hair and a Saville Row suit. He lifted a glass from the tray and held it ready in front of his mouth. He waited for the others to take theirs which they all consumed simultaneously, in one gulp.

"I wasn't sure that you Essex boys was going to be joining us tonight. Not now that you've found…God." He let out a guttural laugh.

"What do you mean?" replied Simon

"Oh, we seen your little video. Everybody's seen your little video. There's no hiding that now, is there Steve?"

The tall, silent, stooping figure next to him giggled. "No, Maxie. It's been all round the office."

"I mean, to be fair," Maxie continued, "that girl can sing. And you guys weren't that bad. I have seen worse." He guffawed, causing his prominent Adam's apple to bob up and down his heavily-veined throat. "But that long-'aired geezer. What do you make of that? Is 'e your mate, is 'e?"

"Mate, erm no, of course not," replied Simon, desperate to divert yet another episode of humiliation from materialising.

"He's no mate of ours!" declared Andy in solidarity. "He's just a guy we met on the train one night and he lets us hang out at his house. He asked us to help him out to do that video. Simon's got the production skills."

"I see," responded Maxie. "So, you don't actually believe in any of that God shit then?"

Simon and Andy shook their heads. Then they looked at each other. Simon felt ashamed and summoned some courage to correct what he had said.

"Actually, Maxie. The guy in the video, the one with the long hair, he *is* my friend, actually. He's called Jez and he's all right."

Andy also felt a tinge of conscience, "Yes, Jez is all right, I guess."

The conversation had reached an awkward impasse. Maxie's face was a picture of disgust. "Come on, let's do our next shot!" he said, almost reluctantly. He raised his clenched fist above the pedestal and waited for the others to do the same. He revelled in his self-appointed role as leader of the pack and the others were too afraid of him to challenge his status. "All right let's go!" They pumped their fists three times then each reached for a drink which they knocked back together.

For the remainder of the evening a veneer of geniality was maintained. However, none of the men felt particularly comfortable with the situation. Maxie felt less inclined than usual to hold the floor with comic accounts of imaginary sexual exploits and there was a sense that the trust that had held this fragile collective together on previous occasions had been fractured.

* * *

Maggie was sitting with Jez at the kitchen table, drinking warm milk at the end of a long day.

Her phone chimed – she had received a text. "It's Si!" she exclaimed happily. "The boys are outside; they've just come back from the City. Is it all right if they come in?"

"Yes of course," replied Jez.

There was a polite knock at the unlocked door and the Simon and Andy entered. "Sorry it's so late, but we really needed to see a couple of friendly faces," said Simon who was still feeling ashamed of denying his friendship with Jez earlier to Maxie and Steve in the bar. He wanted to see him in person simply to reaffirm how much he actually liked him.

Although he had was not experiencing the same sense of neediness, Andy was more than happy to tag along to see Jez and Maggie. "So how are you both doing?"

"We're okay but we had a bit of an upset earlier. Some idiots dumped some barrels full of poison on the farm," replied Jez.

"That's terrible, Jez!" responded Simon sympathetically. "Who would do a thing like that?"

"I don't know. Obviously, somebody who doesn't care about the world like we do."

"So, what do you need to do to get it sorted?"

"It's okay – I've called the council and we are getting it all taken away tomorrow. How about you two? Are you okay?"

Andy and Simon hesitated and looked at each other. Andy spoke. "We've been out on the town with some guys from work. They've seen the video."

"And what did they think?" asked Jez.

"They're not fans. They liked Maggie's singing but they're definitely not into the God stuff!"

"Well I suppose that's a start, anyway," Jez smiled. "How would you fancy making another one tomorrow? Maggie's had an idea, haven't you, Maggie?"

Maggie blushed a little. "Yes, I have. After what happened today, I want us to make a video about looking after the earth. It's so important that we do this for all our futures."

"And you've thought of another song we could use, haven't you Maggie?" She nodded and diffidently lowered her head. "Would you sing it to us please?".

Maggie looked up and saw the three men smiling at her in expectation. She composed herself and began to sing sweetly.

For the beauty of the earth,
For the beauty of the skies,
For the love which from our birth
Over and around us lies.

Chapter 6

Lavinia Finkelstein was struggling to craft her essay – her creative juices were simply not flowing today, and she was yearning for something. An adventure! She was young and she needed to have a proper adventure before life became too complicated.

A high achiever from a successful family, she had fulfilled her family's expectations so far by getting into Harvard and was now close to completing her second year, majoring in Economics. She had made some interesting friends and played flute in the Mozart Society Orchestra. But somehow it felt as though she was merely treading water, waiting to discover what she really wanted to do with her life.

She looked down at her laptop screen and decided to take a little diversion into YouTube. She opened the app and, prominently displayed in her recommendations list, was an unusual looking video which caught her eye. It was entitled 'New Life: A Beautiful World'. There was a picture of some countryside with four interesting faces superimposed. She felt curious and clicked the play button to watch the video.

It began with a catchy drum and bass track. A musician herself, she detected a significant level of ingenuity and originality and she could feel her emotions being aroused. A panorama of beautiful spring outdoor scenes was explored by the camera as additional layers were added to the sound. Then the spoken voices of two young men, with English accents, came in, rapping; their animated faces superimposed over the rustic scenes.

This world is beautiful.
This world is ours.
Let's keep it together.
Get out of your cars.
We need to respect it.
We need to protect it.
We don't want our children
To find that we've wrecked it.

The video switched to pictures of ecological vandalism and the music took a more sombre tone. Smoking barrels of noxious chemical dumped on a farm, bulldozers flattening historic tropical rainforests, sewage pouring into rivers.

The music returned to its original pattern as the video faded over to an image of four people sitting around a table and enjoying each other's company. One was a young woman with striking dark eyes. The camera zoomed in on her and she began to sing to the camera in a clear and soulful mezzo-soprano.

For the beauty of the earth,
For the beauty of the skies,
For the love which from our birth
Over and around us lies

Next the focus turned to an older man who spoke authoritatively

It's time to refocus.
It's time for rebirth.
We need to stop people
destroying our Earth.

There was some more singing and rapping and then this mysterious video ended.

Lavinia loved the fusion of modern dance and sacred music and the simple message resonated with her beliefs. She had been raised in the context of the Jewish faith but had arrived at a personal brand of spirituality which also incorporated aspects of eastern religions, encountered through reading.

She wanted to know more about this video. She looked at the description of the New Life YouTube channel which read as follows.

We are Maggie, Simon, Andy and Jez. A group of friends from Ingatestone in Essex, Great Britain, exploring together how we can live a spiritual life.

We try to follow three simple principles:

- Protecting the planet for ourselves and for those who are yet to come,
- Loving one another, and
- Just doing the next right thing!

It's all about trying to follow your own personal concept of God, if you have one, or, if you don't, to follow the inner voice of your conscience.

Please get in touch with us if you'd like to know more.

Lavinia's plans for the summer vacation, which was due to start in a week's time, had fallen through, due to a relationship break up. On a whim, she decided to head for Ingatestone. Within ten minutes she had arranged her flights, and her Airbnb, and soon she would be on her way with a large rucksack on her back. She just needed to complete that pesky essay first!

* * *

It was a beautiful summer's evening in Ingatestone. The farm had begun to receive a small number of visitors off the back of the release of the two YouTube videos. A few had asked to stay for a while. Some were staying in lodgings in the village while others had put up tents in the fields and were using amenities in the main farmhouse.

Jez managed the farm on behalf of the elderly couple who owned it, and they afforded him a great deal of freedom to use the premises however he saw fit.

On this lovely evening, Jez had invited everybody to an outdoor picnic in the farmhouse garden. He asked that they bring food and refreshments to share with one another. Soon there was a happy throng of over twenty people sitting on the grass, talking happily. Simon and Andy had arrived back from work in London and were winding down and mingling with the friendly outsiders. Among them was another friend of Jez's who had arrived from London. A slightly grizzled looking man in his sixties. Simon and Andy were eager to meet him. Could this be the famous John?

Maggie was still living in the cottage with Jez. It had been several months since she had moved in when her understanding had been that this was to be temporary. But Jez had assured her that there was no urgency for her to leave and both parties were happy to continue with the arrangement.

When the meal was finished, Jez stood up and spoke. "Hello everybody. It's been a lovely picnic. I think I have already met you all and you probably know who I am. You may well recognise some of my friends here from our videos. But I think it would be nice to make a few introductions and ask our guests to do the same. Is that okay?"

There was a general murmur of agreement.

"Right then, I'm Jez, and I'm the farm manager. This is Maggie, who is staying here and helps me out with the day-to-day running of the farm. Over there are Simon and Andy who work up in London and live in the village," indicating the location of his friends with the palm of his outstretched hand.

"I'm also very pleased that my dear friend, John, from London, is here visiting us tonight." He put his arm affectionately around the shoulder of the old man.

"In a minute, I'd like to tell you a bit about what we are trying to do here, and then I will handover to John to say a few words as well. But first I'd like to ask you to tell everybody who you are. Shall we start with the group that are camping here?"

The assorted visitors took it turns to introduce themselves or their parties. There was a group of friends from Cirencester, Aftab, Caroline and Nigel; there was a middle-aged couple from Bath, Sally and Silvia, who wore new-age garments and jewellery; there was an entire family from Holland with three teenage children; and there was a collection of four musicians from Manchester.

Once the introductions were over, Jez spoke again. He talked about the work he did on the farm with Maggie and how important it was to protect the world from harm. He described how he had once led a very different life and how he had been an alcoholic. John had shown him how to turn his life around.

"There are some much bigger problems in the world that we need to tackle urgently if we are going to have a decent future. We've got to stop the destruction of our planet. But first we need to stop fighting among ourselves. We want to start a spiritual revolution that attracts people from all religions, as well as those with no religion, where we all work together to save the Earth." He paused and there was spontaneous applause and cheering, after which he concluded, "Thank you. It means a lot to have your support. And now over to you, John."

John stood up to address the fledgling movement. "Hello friends, it's great to see you all. I really think that this could be the start of something big and we can make some real changes in the world."

"Me and Jez, we go back years. We come from very different backgrounds, me and him, but he's like a little brother to me. I mean that, he *is*, honestly. I've known him since he was a right tearaway, and it's been a great pleasure to see him grow up and put himself to good use.

"I also had my demons in the past. I've been on the wrong side of the law and I've hurt people. But now I live the spiritual life. You know, Jez and I used to spend hours and hours walking along the River Lea and pouring out our hearts to each other. And we got it all out and we dealt with it all and that's what set us free.

"It's great that you've all come here to spend time with Jez and his new mates, and I hope you can help them make the world a bit better."

But before John had a chance to wrap up his address, he was interrupted by the noise of an approaching vehicle. Heads turned to see a taxi pulling up in the lane in front of the farm. A statuesque, blond lady, wearing shorts and a tee-shirt, climbed out and retrieved a huge rucksack from inside, which she hoisted onto her back. She walked up to the gate. Lavinia had arrived in Ingatestone.

Chapter 7

The following evening was even warmer. Once again all had gathered in the garden with the new addition of the confident young lady from across the Atlantic.

Lavinia had enjoyed her first evening at the farm immensely. Perhaps she had drunk a little too much wine and warm English beer, but she already felt a strong sense of belonging here.

It had been exciting to meet Jez and his friends from the YouTube videos in the flesh. Jez had been an excellent host, and she had found him to be warm and attractive. Simon had seemed rather shy whereas Andy was clearly something of a show-off who had enjoyed putting his cheeky Essex charm to use in trying to impress her. She felt like she was going to become good friends with all three of them.

Maggie, however, had seemed a little offhand. Lavinia had tried to put her at her ease by complimenting her on her singing voice and good looks. But there was something slightly hostile about her body language that had made the hairs on the back of Lavinia's neck stand up.

This evening, she was once again breezing around confidently. The group of Mancunian musicians were playing folk-rock songs: two men playing guitar, a female violinist and another female singing and playing a tambourine. Lavinia approached them.

"Hey! I love what you're playing. I have my flute here in my bag. Do you think I could join in with you?"

The musicians smiled. They looked toward the violinist who seemed to be the de facto leader of the band. "Why sure, love," she replied. "Come and sit next to me."

Lavinia sat down, as suggested, and started to play along, quite tentatively at first. She was usually in the habit of performing classical music but liked to experiment with other genres and could play by ear. Before long she felt confident to harmonise and improvise, careful to hold back sufficiently to remain in a supporting role and not to alienate the rest of the band by showing off.

Lavinia joining with the band acted as a catalyst for a small and enthusiastic audience forming and joining in with the songs. After a while, though, hunger kicked in, and the group decided to begin their picnic. Lavinia made a beeline to sit with Jez, who was again with his friend John. She talked about her concerns regarding ecology, starvation and illness, citing examples of wrongdoing by major corporations and governments causing death and destruction.

"We really can't carry on like this, you know. All our wealth and prosperity is tainted by investment links to unethical activities: trading arms with rogue states, and destructive farming practices that are threatening the survival of remote tribes and rare species of animals. If only everybody would follow the three principles of your New Life movement."

Jez and John listened quietly and attentively, clearly impressed with her passion. She seemed to Jez to be somebody with great potential to help with his cause. "Lavinia, I am just blown away that you came all this way to stay with us. Your knowledge and enthusiasm will be invaluable."

Jez and Lavinia were clearly very much at ease with each other. John was starting to feel left out, and his eyes began to wander around the garden. Soon he noticed another woman, sitting alone, looking anxiously towards Jez and Lavinia, who was being very tactile with him. He instinctively sensed her insecurity, so he made his excuses and walked over to her.

"Hello Maggie. Mind if I join you?"

She smiled at him. "Of course not, John. Go ahead."

* * *

Jez and John were strolling along Hall Lane to the Station in the twilight at the end of another stimulating evening with the burgeoning New Life group. They were quickly getting down to the crux of things, just as they always did, having walked, as John had said earlier, many, many a mile together pouring their hearts out. They had no secrets from each other.

John was essentially Jez's spiritual advisor, but such was the strength of their relationship that, on many occasions, they had found the roles being reversed.

"Things are beginning to happen here, Jez. It's really exciting. You've got a real gift with people. You can stir up their passion. I always knew you had something special about you. And I think that what you've started here is really taking off."

"Thanks, John. I've got an awful lot to thank you for. I hate to think what would have happened if I hadn't met you."

"That's my pleasure, mate. You've got to give it away if you want to keep it!" John paused and took a deep breath. "Just be careful, though. You was in a lot of trouble a few years ago with that fraud case. You was lucky you didn't end up in the nick with them blokes you worked with. And bankers have got long memories! Just be careful that what we are doing now doesn't stir up any trouble from the past."

"I guess I'll just have to cross that bridge when I come to it, John. I'm living on a different plane now. I am trying to do God's will, not enslaved to money or to alcohol."

"Okay, mate. Just take care. And remember I'm always here for you."

"I know that, John. And I am here for you too."

John had a burning question on his mind. "By the way. Sorry, but I've got to ask this. What's going on with you and Maggie? People are wondering whether you two are a couple. I know you took her in to get

43

her off drugs and off the street. But she's still there and I think she's into you."

"Oh, you know me, John. I'm celibate." Jez laughed.

John gently put a hand on Jez's shoulder. "I know we've talked about all this and everything that happened. But it doesn't always have to be this way, you know."

"I don't want to take advantage of her and frankly… I would be a bit scared of getting into a relationship with her."

"But maybe you deserve some happiness too, Jez. Maybe you do. Just think about that."

At the station, the two men stood together on the platform until the London train arrived. Without any trace of self-consciousness, they hugged each other hard in front of the other passengers. Then John stepped onboard.

∗ ∗ ∗

Jez entered the cottage and noticed Maggie sitting with her elbows on the table and her hands on her brow. She looked troubled.

"Are you okay, Maggie?"

"Not really."

Jez walked over and sat next to her.

"I'm feeling confused. I mean, what's going on? With us? I'm still living here. This was just meant to be temporary, but I'm still here. Where's it going?"

"Maggie, I've always been on my own, you know. I brought you here to help you. I didn't want to take advantage. I really do like having you here, though."

She became very agitated. "But what if I wanted you to take advantage? Do you like me that way? Do you even *like* women? How would you feel if I was with somebody else? Si or Andy, say. Not that I would, though. Would that bother you?"

Jez paused and carefully considered what to say next. His code was never to tell lies, but he didn't want to make any false promises either. "Yes, it would," he replied. "Listen, Maggie, there are some things about me you don't know yet. Nothing too heavy. But I come with a lot of baggage. And anybody who got into a relationship with me would need to be able to handle that."

* * *

One of the most exhilarating adventures of a young life is to become part of a new tribe – meeting a diverse group of strangers with whom you can instantly bond and it feels like your life has changed forever. Beautiful vistas of a possible future open before you. It all feels so meaningful and you never lose those wonderful memories.

Three weeks later Lavinia was striding confidently up to the front door of Jez's cottage. She had now formed a strong bond with members of the group. It had been an enjoyable time for her, passing many happy evenings in good company. Further visitors had been arriving from near and far, some of whom showed no desire to leave. More videos had been created and new members of the movement had become familiar to subscribers to the New Life YouTube channel. Lavinia herself had collaborated on the musical side, contributing some improvised and expressive flute solos to Simon's compositions and adding backing vocals to Maggie's lead.

She knocked on the door and went in. Jez was at the table with Maggie, Simon and Andy, chatting and drinking tea.

"Hi Lavinia. Nice to see you. Would you like to come and sit with us?" he asked.

The seating arrangements still consisted of upturned crates and Andy stood up and gave her his, which she politely accepted and sat down.

"It's good that you are all here," she said. "I've got something I want to propose to you all."

Andy looked across at Simon and winked. "That sounds interesting," he said cheekily.

Lavinia decided against entering into any casual banter: sometimes when you've got something important to say it's best just to get on with it and not be distracted.

"I've got a business proposal that I want to pitch to you. I haven't told you any of this before and please keep it to yourselves for now." The friends saw that she was serious and nodded their agreement. "I... actually come from an extremely wealthy family in New York. I have a lot of powerful connections and I've been trying to think of a way that I might be able to help."

She looked at all the faces present to ensure that she had their attention and continued. "I think you've started something really great here. That blend of rap, dance and sacred music. It opens the door for you to get your message across.

"Anyway, this is what I am proposing. We will get the music professionally produced and released onto iTunes. Then we will set up a not-for-profit company called the New Life Corporation and we will use the profits from the music, of which there will be plenty I can assure you, to pay for your expenses and to enable you to do good things with the money that's left over."

"Wow!" said Simon, almost bursting with pride at the idea of his music hobby and naff rapping turning into something professional. "That sounds amazing. Do you really think you can do that?"

"For sure! Yes, I believe I can," replied Lavinia.

"Now hold on a minute!" interjected Andy. "I don't want to be the party pooper, but how do we know we can trust you? I mean we've only known you for a few weeks. What's in it for you? What kind of contacts do you actually have?"

"Shush, Andy," said Simon, embarrassed.

"No, it's okay, let me answer that, Si. I understand why Andy asked that. I want to do this because I really believe in what we stand for. I'm lucky enough to have some money and I want to put it to good use. I really don't want to see the Earth getting destroyed and just stand by and let it happen.

"All decisions regarding the New Life Corporation will be made by you guys exclusively – you will have complete control of what happens. I will just act as an advisor and business manager. As for my contacts – my family runs a major portfolio of businesses and investments spread across quite a few different sectors."

"I think this could be an incredibly good opportunity for us, Lavinia. Thank you," said Jez. Now you three, Simon, Andy and Maggie, need to decide whether it's right for you. Bear in mind that you would be handing over the rights to the music you've been making to this corporation to use rather than keeping it for yourselves. How would you feel about that?"

Simon, who was not remotely deterred, was the first to speak. "Seriously! Is this seriously going to happen? I'm well up for it. Thank you, Lavinia."

"Well if Si is for it, so am I," followed Andy, loyal as always to his best friend. "After all, he's the brains behind what he and I do. What do you think, Maggie?"

Maggie was not a great fan of Lavinia. She saw her a potential obstacle to any future relationship she might have with Jez. Her life had been so easy, everything given to her on a plate. She had just sauntered over here on a whim and now it seemed that she was planning to take over the whole New Life movement. And everybody seemed to have forgotten that it had been Maggie who had come up with that name.

But on the other hand, she had enjoyed making music with Lavinia and certainly wished her no ill will. This proposal would mean that her voice would be heard all over the world and the money could be used to help with Jez's plans.

She hesitated for a while and finally muttered "I think it sounds… wonderful."

* * *

The late-night Central Line train was virtually empty as it rattled noisily towards Bethnal Green Tube Station. John had spent another lovely evening with Jez and his friends in Ingatestone. He had become a frequent visitor to the farm of late, several times a week when funds allowed for the train fare. Tonight's

48

meeting had been very uplifting, and the New Life music tracks were proving popular on iTunes, in several countries. Not a lot of money coming in yet but definitely heading in the right direction. He was standing up by the door – too excited to sit down.

He noticed a couple of shifty looking men sitting nearby. Hadn't he seen them already on the platform at Stratford? They appeared to be eyeing him for some reason!

The train pulled into his stop, he disembarked and started to walk briskly in the direction of the exit. Glancing anxiously over his shoulder, he saw that the two men were following closely behind him. One was a small wiry man in a grey suit and the other was tall and gangly. He felt an acute sense of danger in the air. He said to himself, "Come on, John, stay calm and think about what a great evening you've had."

He fumbled with his ticket as he used it to pass through the barrier. He realised that there was nobody else in view except for the two men, who now quickened their step.

"Hello, John," said one as the three men walked into an empty side road.

"Erm, who are you?" replied John.

"You don't know us, but we know you. It's not very nice, I know, but we need to teach a lesson to your long-'aired mate and all 'is hippies."

Before he could say a word, a swipe to his ankle dropped him to the ground and the two men viciously kicked him in his rib cage and head repeatedly.

"That's enough, Maxie," exhorted Steve. "He's had enough. He's stopped moving." The two thugs looked around and disappeared into the night, leaving John's lifeless body behind on the pavement.

Chapter 8

There was a subdued tone to the gathering the following evening. As soon as the group had all arrived, Jez stood up and addressed them with a heavy heart.

"My friends. I am sure by now you have all heard about the cowardly attack on my dear friend, John, yesterday evening on his way back from here. He was savagely beaten in the street and his life is now hanging in the balance. I went to visit him in the Royal London Hospital this afternoon. He has been placed in an induced coma while tests are carried out on his brain function. Now we can only hope and pray that he will pull through."

There was an angry murmur in the group. Jez continued.

"This might not have been just a random attack. It's possible that we have been targeted. We have been getting quite a lot of publicity lately through our New Life channel and corporation. I need to make you aware that our mission to protect the planet might be seen as a threat. There are those who hate what we stand for. They will seek to destroy us if they perceive that their financial interests are at risk.

"So please be careful! We will be persecuted — these are powerful enemies! If anybody wants to leave that would be understandable."

A few of the group looked at each other to assess the overall mood. Some seemed angry and defiant. Others simply sad. For one or two present, the savage assault on John had been a reality check which would soon see them scuttling back to the relative safety and obscurity of their old lives.

"From now on we need to take a few extra precautions. Please stay close to one another. Don't walk back to the village on your own. I will take you back to the houses where you are staying in the Land Rover.

"Also, and I know this is hard, try not to hate the people that did this terrible thing to John. Just hate what they did. Because if we hate people, then we will be less useful in sorting out the problems in the world.

"Finally, remember how important the work that we are doing is. It is about the future of the whole world, our children and our children's children. Let's try to have a good time tonight. Tomorrow is another day. We haven't lost John yet. He's a tough old sod! Let's enjoy some good music and some good food together."

Jez sat together with Simon, Andy, Maggie and Lavinia. Instinctively they reached for each other's hands. This was the core of the movement. These were the people who had made the biggest personal commitment. They all made an effort to stay positive and be strong for each other.

* * *

Later, Maggie and Jez returned to the cottage.

"You spoke well, Jez. You said what needed to be said tonight."

She noticed a tear trickling down his face from the corner of his eye. She held him tenderly and kissed him gently on his bearded cheek. Jez hugged her and

51

soon they were kissing each other's lips. Maggie started to pull him over towards her bed. But Jez hesitated. "You know I told you I come with a lot of baggage."

Maggie reassured him. "Don't worry. We love each other. We are going to be just fine."

Chapter 9

Five men dressed in colourful, hooded robes were sitting around a pentagonal, carved oak table, talking and gesticulating worriedly. They had travelled from various locations around the World to meet in this secret chamber within the vaults of Chillon Castle, situated on Lake Geneva.

Their conversation was interrupted by the cantor ringing his handbell. He waited for silence and then commenced to sing the ancient Roman battle cry.

> *Sive sequimur aquilas*
> *Sive progredimur ad cornices soli*
> *Nostra superbia est in legione*
> *Et pugnans peditatus est domus gensque*

The seated men joined him to repeat the final line with gusto.

> *Et pugnans peditatus est domus gensque*

At this point the cantor and servants left the room, leaving only the five core members of the ancient order. Maddocks, a slight, bespectacled man in his eighties, rose from his chair to address the others with a formal greeting.

"*Salvete, fratres!*"

"*Salve, Domine!*" came the reply.

"G'day. Thanks a lot for coming along tonight, you blokes," he continued in an Antipodean accent. "What do you think of our Swiss hospitality? I don't know about you, but I'm bloody loving it." There was an impatient murmur of approval as he raised a heavy jewelled goblet to his lips and took a slug of vintage red.

"Very well, let's get on with it. Without further ado, I declare this extraordinary meeting of the ancient brotherhood of the Praefecti started. Now, as I am sure you know, we have only the one very important item of business to discuss tonight. And that is the threat posed by a certain Jez Lamb and his 'New Life Corporation'.

"It seems that young Lamb has set himself up as some kind of 'Save the Planet' guru over in England. At first, we thought he was just a harmless loony," he chuckled. "However, things have begun to get a bit more serious.

"Now, you might ask, you might ask me, if you didn't know me any better, 'Rufus, why was it bloody necessary to take us all away from our cosy lives and bring us all the bloody way over here to talk about a bunch of bloody drop-outs?' After all, their so-called New Life Corporation looks like it's just a handful of hippies, singing happy-clappy protest songs about trees, and trying to sell them online. The songs, not the trees.

"I mean, they've barely got ten thousand followers on their social media channel, which is nothing, is it Gately? Nothing! And the sales of their music are modest at best.

"However, since Lamb set up this corporation, he and his cronies have been sticking their noses into high places and are gaining influence. Aaron Finkelstein has switched forty per cent of his personal holdings to ethical investments. And he's buying up the rainforest like there's no tomorrow. What a drongo!

"His granddaughter is tied up in this sect and he's got a soft spot for her. Funny thing is…the stocks he's bought have been soaring, abso..bloody..lutely soaring! Now all the other big players are considering following suit. Can you believe it?

"What's more, he's got a plan for his rainforest holdings too. You've heard of bitcoin – well…welcome to the…'finkelcoin'!

"Yes, it's true, a little dicky bird has told us that old Finkie' has created a new currency – one square foot of unspoilt rainforest equals one finkelcoin. If this takes off with currency traders, if the price goes too high, well…it could wipe out many of our assets.

"Big-time disruption! This poses a major threat to our power base and everything we have stood for over the past seven centuries. We need to act fast and nip this in the bud. People aren't really so bothered about the rainforest anymore, are they? As long as it doesn't affect them, they turn a blind eye to it. We just need to create some seriously bad publicity for Lamb and the Finkelsteins.

"So, tell us, what did we find out about Lamb, Brother Abelman?"

Maddocks took his seat and Abelman immediately sprung from his. He was a sprightly man in his fifties with jet back hair, a former secret services commander. He systematically and confidently made eye contact with each man present, in his mind

54

asserting his physical superiority, before starting his address.

"As you all know, I have been gathering intelligence from my contacts in London. Let me recap. It would appear that Lamb is not quite what he seems. He used to be a senior trader with Freeman Baldwin. And he was quite the wild man – a constant fixture on the London party scene, always with a drink in his hand, cocaine up his nose, and a stunning brunette dripping off his arm. He was the star trader and he could do whatever he liked with very little scrutiny.

"Then he got a conscience. Cleaned up his act… He blew the whistle to the regulators concerning some fraud scandal that was responsible for major environmental harm. Almost brought down the bank! They had to broker a deal to keep this all out of the public eye. Cost them a fortune!"

"Anyway, he was tried secretly alongside his colleagues. All hushed up. He was let off with a suspended sentence in return for his continued silence. Others were not so lucky – so he has his share of enemies.

"Just one final point I want to make. What Lamb knows is dynamite, absolute dynamite! This kind of stuff is going on everywhere. In the current climate, he could bring down the entire edifice. If he were to spill the beans, it would play right into the hands of the likes of Finkelstein and his neo-socialist friends. The whole political landscape of the world could change rapidly. There would be chaos and we would lose out big time!"

There were some brief questions and answers. Maddocks waited until he felt sure that the assembled group had reached a common understanding of the situation and then spoke again.

"Thank you, Brother Abelman. Now I'd like to hand over to Brother Maximov. Tell us your proposal for how we should deal with this little problem we are facing, please."

Maximov, a portly and balding former Russian General, rose to his feet. He did not possess such a high level of proficiency in spoken English as his colleagues, so he kept his message simple and to the point.

"We must destabilise the New Life Corp. Without Lamb they are nothing. We must discredit him. Break his support base. Gately can help with that. Then, with people turning against him, we will take him out of the game. He will disappear!" As he finished speaking, he made a chopping motion with his right hand. Seeing no indication that any of his colleagues wished to speak, he sat and pointed a finger towards Gately to signify that it was his turn to address the meeting.

At first, Gately seemed a little taken aback to have had the spotlight turned on him so abruptly. Then he smiled smugly and began to speak excitedly, with a lyrical Texan drawl. "We can inject negative memes into his supporters' social media feeds!" He remembered he should have been standing. "Sorry, Brother Maddocks. Would you like me to speak on this now?" Maddocks nodded his head and signalled him to recommence with an upwards flick of the hand. Gately hauled his tall and awkward body from his seat, spread out his huge sweaty hands on the tabletop, leaned forward, and continued.

"Gentlemen, let me explain. We have the power and the technology to get inside people's heads. We can directly target Lamb's followers. We can attack them on two fronts. Both their conscious and the sub-conscious minds.

"Let's start with how we can control their conscious minds. We can apply advanced analytics to the usage data that we retrieve from their personal devices to understand exactly what makes them tick: what they like and what they don't like. Then we can insert targeted stories into their online newsfeeds. We are messing directly with their conscious minds. And remember, we don't only have to rely just on fake news. We've dug up enough dirt on Lamb to destroy his reputation for good!

"Now, when it comes to their subconscious minds the approach is a bit more subtle. Whenever they are working on their devices, or watching videos, we will make little messages flash up for a split second to give them some false information about Lamb. Their conscious minds will have absolutely no idea that this has happened. But the subconscious mind sees everything! The messages will go deep into their memory nonetheless and we can start to control their beliefs and opinions!

"Using this technology, we can destroy Lamb's reputation. Finkelstein will be forced to denounce him and rescue his granddaughter. The New Life Corporation will founder and gradually things will return to normal!"

Gately sat back down, feeling very satisfied with this explanation.

"Yes, yes, we've all seen how you've done this before to swing elections and referendums. It's bloody clever stuff! Simply bloody marvellous!" replied Maddocks. "We will and we must use that technology. But it's not enough on its own. None of that can take away the inside knowledge that Lamb possesses which could blow the doors off everything we stand for. He could use that to absolutely shaft us. We've got to take him out! There is no other way. Let me turn it over to you, Brother Rothman."

A stout man, with a long lank hair, thick glasses, and a huge porcine face, slowly elevated his heavy frame and spoke in a high-pitched, cut-glass English accent. "Don't worry. We have that in hand. Despite it not being one of ours, I do, of course, have a couple of insiders in the bank that will take care of it for us. They know Lamb from the old days and have some unfinished business with him.

"I have already used them to put the frighteners on the group and they were extremely discreet. They hate Lamb's guts, blame him for ruining a very lucrative venture that would have made them extremely rich. He singlehandedly wrecked both their lives.

"There is no way to trace any of us from them. If they get caught the police will simply assume that it was a vendetta related to their previous history together."

"Wonderful," said Maddocks. "Are there are any questions for Rothman? No? Okay you can take a seat again, mate.

"So, let's see a show of hands. All those in favour of taking out Lamb… Motion carried unanimously!

"Unless there is any further business, I will close this meeting now." He looked around the table and saw that everyone was content to end the discussion, so he rang his handbell to summon back the servants to serve liqueurs and cigars. The remainder of the evening passed cordially, and the five men returned to their respective hotels in due course without incident.

Chapter 10

Jez was repairing a damaged gate in the field immediately next to the farmhouse garden when he spotted Lavinia striding across the grass towards him beneath the overcast sky. The farm had been busy with the harvest over the past few weeks and the summer was drawing to its end. Most of the campers had disappeared from the farm by now and only a handful of visitors remained in Ingatestone as part of the New Life group.

Lavinia arrived and spoke to Jez. After exchanging some initial pleasantries, she came to the point. "Jez, I really need to talk to you. We've got a problem!"

"Yes, of course, Lavinia," he replied. "Let's head over to the farmhouse and discuss."

They strolled over to the house and went into the kitchen where Jez made a pot of tea. Once it was ready, he poured them both out a large refreshing mug and they sat down together by the kitchen table. "Okay, so what's up?" he asked.

"Have you seen what's been happening on Facebook and YouTube? There are stories about you all over it. I think that's why people have started to leave the group. You really need to see this."

Jez watched as she pulled out her phone and showed him her YouTube feed. At the top of the list of recommended videos was one entitled 'Jez Lamb – Hippy or Hypocrite?' There was a picture of him, from years before, standing in bar, smartly dressed, glass in hand, clutching an attractive woman.

Another picture showed bulldozers clearing land in the rainforest and a third picture appeared to show indigenous forest dwellers looking on aghast at the destruction of their land.

Lavinia looked at Jez with concerned eyes. "Please play it?" he asked quietly. She obliged him and they watched the video together. It was framed like an official news programme, starting with a reporter in Ingatestone High Street, describing the New Life group as a new-age cult. Then flashing back to various pictures of Jez's younger days interspersed with interviews, supposedly with former colleagues. They provided detailed accounts of outrageous drunken behaviour and drug taking.

Then there was a section about his former career at the Freeman Baldwin investment bank. Jez was said to have been instrumental in funding a Palm Oil start-up company which had been responsible for widescale deforestation in Papau New Guinea, destroying the ancestral homes of several tribes and threatening the survival of several endangered species of animals. The video ended with another shot of the reporter who ended by saying, "So who is the real Jez Lamb? Saint or charlatan?"

Jez sorrowfully buried his head in his hands. Lavinia put her arm around his shoulder and tried to comfort him.

"Look, I'm sure this isn't real, Jez," she said. "Our enemies are trying to destroy us because we're raising people's awareness all over the world. But this is really hurting us." She composed herself and then spoke calmly, "Jez, tell me this isn't true."

He raised his head to look at her and said, "Lavinia…I'm afraid that most of this *is* true. You know that I was once addicted to drink and it's also true that I abused cocaine. When I was working for the bank, I was reckless. I took some shortcuts to feed my habit.

"I was approached by a representative from a Palm Oil production company, called Midas, and I invested the bank's money and also raised funds from some very prominent investors, without carrying out proper 'due diligence' checks.

"Anyway, the shares rocketed in value and I recruited loads of additional investors, including some very well-known establishment figures. I was flavour of the month – everybody wanted a piece of me.

"Unfortunately, and unknown to me, it transpired that Midas was operating both illegally and unethically. They were forging land sale certificates for vast areas of the rainforest using the names of tribal elders who had died, and then they were burning the forests and evicting the tribes from their homelands. I really didn't know about any of this at the time. I was too busy feeding my addiction.

"One day I was called into a board meeting and I was told what was going on and that I had to keep my mouth shut – or else! I couldn't live with myself. I quit my job and I went on a massive binge of drink and drugs and hoped that I wouldn't survive. But somehow, I did survive.

"Then, one night, I had an incredibly vivid dream, one that I will never forget. I dreamed that I was running through a burning forest, trying to escape from the flames and smoke. Running alongside me were lots of terrified little furry animals, the likes of which I had never seen before.

"I came into a clearing and saw a little grass hut on stilts. Standing in front of it was a family of four, wearing tribal costumes. They all reached out to me and the father spoke. 'You can help us, if you want to.' 'Of course, I want to,' I replied.

"I awoke in a sweat and suddenly realised that I wanted to live, after all, and that, most of all, I wanted to make up for the harm that I had done!

"I went into recovery and that's how I met John. He helped me to set about putting right the wrongs from my past. And that meant I would have to try to take down this Midas company who had been stealing the land from the tribes in New Guinea.

"I went to the Financial Conduct Authority and told them everything I knew. Lots of people in high places were implicated. It was all hushed up because the scandal would have been too great for the country to bear. But, eventually, Midas got shut down and their business was taken over by a more ethical, but much less profitable, one.

"So, this is what drives me on now. I happen to know that there are many other organisations like Midas out there, harming the world irretrievably. We can try to fight them, but I think that the real answer lies in education and spiritual enlightenment.

"Lavinia, you must keep this to yourself – these are *very* dangerous things to know."

Lavinia carefully mulled over what Jez had told her. "So, in the end you managed to stop this company from continuing with their destructive ways?"

"Yes, but I only found out about this because of the greed that led me to invest in the first place without checking them out properly. I was still implicated in the harm that was done," he replied.

"Jez, I understand. And I still believe in you. We can get through this. I have some good and trustworthy contacts in the cyber intelligence world that can help us to track down where this campaign is coming from and to combat this."

"Thank you, Lavinia," he replied. "I think I need to talk to our supporters. I will organise a Zoom meeting for all our subscribers, tomorrow evening."

*   *   *

The door to the public bar of the Bell Public House in Ingatestone High Street swung open and two well-dressed figures marched in and stepped towards the bar.

"What can I get you, gents?" asked the landlady.

"Get us a both a Jack Daniels and coke, Darling," said the smaller of the men. "Maxie's the name – this is my amigo, Steve." They sat on a couple of vacant bar stools and made some small talk with her. A rather unkempt man was sitting across the bar from them, staring morosely into a half-drunk pint of cider.

"So, what do you make of this cult that's started up around here?" asked Maxie.

"Well they seem all right to me. As long as they keep themselves to themselves, I'm not bothered," replied the landlady. "But you should talk to this chap, here. You're one of them Hippies, ain't you, darling?"

"Not really. I'm just hanging around here for the summer because I've got nothing better to do," replied the young man in a West Country accent.

"So, you're not from around here, son?" asked Maxie.

"No, I'm from Cirencester."

"What's your name, mate?" asked Steve.

"I'm Nigel."

"I'm Steve and this is Maxie. Very pleased to meet you, mate." They all shook hands. "It's lovely over in your neck of the woods, isn't it? We don't live here either. Just driving through. Why don't the three of us go and sit at a table outside and have a nice chat. What are you drinking, mate?"

"Well, if you're buying, I'll have what you're having. Thanks a lot."

"Three more JD and cokes, darling," said Maxie to the landlady. As soon as the drinks were ready, the men went outside and took a table at the end of the beer garden out of earshot from the other drinkers.

"Now tell us, Nigel son, what do you make of this Jez geezer? Bit of a slag if you ask me," remarked Maxie.

"You are not wrong there, Maxie," replied Nigel. "Goes around preaching about peace and love and God and then it turns out he's done all these really dodgy things. And you know he took in this homeless girl to look after her, and he's properly shacked up with her. Taking advantage of her, you know! I ain't got no time for him at all. No wonder my mates have gone back home to Cirencester."

"You must be feeling really let down by him, son," Maxie continued. "I mean, what's he ever done for you? Look at you. What a mess!"

"You're right," admitted Nigel.

"Now look here, Nigel. We are actually former associates of this Jez. We need to see him on a matter of urgent business. Do you think you could get him to come over here tonight? We'd make it well worth your while." Maxie pulled out a large wad of £50 notes from the inside pocket of his jacket. "Do you want me to give you this, mate? All you've gotta do is give him a call and tell him to come and meet you here urgently. All right?"

Nigel took out his mobile phone and made the call. "Jez, it's Nigel. I'm here in the garden at The Bell having a drink with a couple of your old friends. Yeah, they're, um, Maxie and Steve – they'd love to see you. Could you come over here right away, please?"

"Cheers, mate," said Maxie. Nigel grabbed the money and headed off briskly.

* * *

Jez arrived at The Bell. He had been expecting a visit sooner or later. He walked gingerly into the beer garden where Maxie and Steve were waiting for him. "Hello, Jez," said Maxie "It's been a while. We're parked around the back. Come on – let's go."

Chapter 11

As his early evening train pulled out of Ingatestone Station, Nigel peeped nervously out of the window to check whether there were any familiar faces on the platform. Reassured that his exit had gone unnoticed, he sat back in his seat, pulled one of the four bottles of Kopparberg cider he had just purchased from his backpack, removed the cap and begun to swig greedily from its neck. He was on his way back home, planning to catch the 9:33 train from Paddington to Kemble.

He counted his money one more time. Twenty folded, and somewhat tatty, fifty-pound notes. It would have been a bad idea to have risked going back to the farm to collect his belongings. Anyway, all he had left behind was a tiny single-berth tent, a sleeping bag and a few clothes.

The cider was going down nicely and, together with the drinks he had already consumed in The Bell, it was taking the edge off any pangs of guilt that he might have been feeling, having summoned Jez there under false pretences to meet the shady characters who had accosted him. What had they wanted with him? They had seemed quite scary and the fact that they had been prepared to pay him so much simply to call Jez appeared to suggest that they had bad intentions. Well, it was no skin off his nose. He felt let down by Jez. He had watched those videos on social media which proved he was a hypocrite!

With another gulp of cider, he put the matter to the back of his mind and decided to look at his phone and listen to some music. His media feed contained a suggestion to play a video by Ed Sheeran, who was one of his favourite artists. He immediately thought back to his set at Glastonbury in '17. He had been there with Aftab. What a weekend that had been!

The video that had come up on his phone was called 'London Bridge', a duet with Yelawolf. He shut his eyes and immersed himself in the track. It began with some rapping, not in Ed's voice, so that must have been Yelawolf. He was telling a very sad story about a man who had lost everything and couldn't stop drinking. Then the chorus began with Ed singing.

London Bridge is falling down, falling down.
And if it don't stop falling then all of us will drown.

Nigel began to visualise himself flying over London Bridge as a bird, soaring in the air over London. Next, he saw himself as a fish happily swimming in the water around the pillars of the bridge, flipping into the air and back down to the water. When the song was finished, he experienced a powerful sense of elation, better than any drug he had ever taken. The track had really got into his head.

He closed his eyes for a second – there seemed to be a message written on the back of his eyelids, lit up like a neon sign which read, 'Come into the water'. How strange! He opened his eyes and closed them again, but the message was still there. Never mind – he was feeling great and he had a big wad of money in his pocket.

He realised that he had never actually been to London Bridge. It couldn't be all that far from Liverpool Street station. Hmmm, perhaps he could take a walk over there before catching the tube to Paddington. He could always catch a later train back to Kemble, if necessary.

* * *

Maxie, Steve and Jez were heading along the A414 towards Harlow in a fairly innocuous BMW 3 series. It had tinted glass windows so that nobody could see inside. Steve was driving, with Maxie and Jez sitting in the back.

Maxie had been planning to coerce Jez into getting into the car at The Bell by threatening to hurt Maggie, but Jez had been surprisingly compliant, almost as if he knew what was going to happen. He had entered the car without raising the suspicions of any onlookers. After travelling in silence to the hamlet of Nine Ashes, they had pulled over in a layby where Jez had been gagged and handcuffed. Now Maxie was holding a pistol, and stroking Jez's temples with it.

"I'd better take your phone," he snapped, pulling Jez's mobile from his pocket. Then he switched it off, wound down his door window, and chucked it out into a hedge. "Don't want nobody tracking this do we, son?"

Maxie had been building up to speak at some length. He began with an air of fake pity, looking directly at Jez who also turned his head to glance serenely back at him.

"You should've kept your 'ead down, son. You could've carried on playing the country boy for the rest of your life and we would've left you alone."

Jez looked into Maxie's eyes with compassion while saying a silent prayer to himself, asking for guidance and for the power to forgive Maxie and Steve. Maxie continued to speak, but now with some genuine hostility.

"Why the hell did you have to blow the whistle on us in the first place? We had it made. We was a team. You, me and Steve. We would've been set up for life. But you had to go and ruin it for all of us. If you had only kept your mouth shut, we could have all been spending our days counting out our money on yachts. We was untouchable!

"There was too many people in the establishment that we could have brought down, lords, bishops, politicians! But you had to destroy it all, didn't you? Little goody two shoes, Jez Lamb.

"You was lucky to get away with it then. But we've been watching you. And you just couldn't help sticking your nose in where it wasn't wanted. You was told to keep it shut! People 'ave done time for you, you slag! Now you're gonna have to pay the price!"

Jez remained calm and his eyes showed no sign of either the fear or anger that Maxie had hoped to induce. "Oh, I can't cope with this. You're trying to make me feel bad," he shouted, temporarily engulfed with unfamiliar feelings of shame that he usually managed to keep suppressed. He slapped Jez's face half-heartedly with the pistol. Then he fumbled around in the foot aisle and brought up a canvas bag which he placed over Jez's head.

The journey continued in silence. Soon they reached the Hastingwood roundabout and sped off towards rural Hertfordshire.

∗ ∗ ∗

Nigel had arrived at London Bridge on foot from Liverpool Street Station. He had drunk the remaining three bottles of his cider during the journey and was feeling decidedly inebriated. He was disappointed to discover that this was actually a somewhat non-descript bridge; he was surprised that it was so famous. He could see Tower Bridge along the river to his left, lit up in the darkness. Now that was a proper bridge!

He gazed at the brightly lit buildings all around him in the London skyline and decided to play that Ed Sheeran track through his earphones again, the one which had inspired him to come here.

The words of the chorus began again.

London Bridge is falling down, falling down.
And if it don't stop falling then all of us will drown.

Nigel flung his arms out and began to run around, making birdlike flapping motions, acting out the scene he had visualised on the train earlier. There were a handful of passers-by who looked on anxiously but said nothing. They had no idea what he was listening to.

As the song reached its climax, Nigel climbed onto the side wall and looked down into the swirling river below. Suddenly his thoughts turned to Jez. He had betrayed him. Placed him in serious danger for money!

Deep down, he had always known that Jez was compassionate and kind. This summer in Ingatestone had been the best of his life.

An immense sense of self-hatred engulfed him. There was simply no choice. Tears were streaming down his face as he disappeared over the side headfirst and plunged into the deep water below. Not a strong swimmer, he made little attempt to save himself. Soon his lungs had filled with water and his body sunk to the bed of the river.

Chapter 12

Lavinia, Simon and Andy were sitting around the table in the cottage with Maggie. They were concerned about Jez – he had not been seen since he had answered a call that afternoon in front of Maggie. Now his phone was turned off and they had no idea where he could be.

It was nearly 9pm, time for the scheduled Zoom meeting, which Lavinia had set up. In light of the recent cyber campaign against Jez, she had enlisted the help of some ethical hackers to keep an eye on things.

"What will we do if he's not here?" asked Simon.

They all felt panicked. There had been a campaign of negative information circulating about their leader, which had started to seriously deplete their following. Now they were expecting their inner circle to join the meeting, a carefully chosen group of key allies from around the world. It was meant to be a chance for Jez to inspire them and to reassure them about those stories that they would surely have heard about his past.

This was a pivotal moment for the future survival of the New Life movement, and the corporation which they had formed to promote ethical commerce and spiritual principles in order to help protect the world. How would it look if he did not actually turn up at this crucial juncture?

"Lavinia…you're gonna have to stand in for Jez," said Andy firmly.

"Yes," agreed Maggie, putting aside any personal rivalry for the sake of the cause. "It has to be you."

Lavinia looked at the other three. Until this point she had felt like something of an outsider, having been a late arrival. She had joined the movement under her own steam, making the trip across the Atlantic specifically to do so, whereas the other three had been personally selected by Jez. And now they were looking to her for leadership at the most critical moment of the movement's short history.

She looked at the three of them, a couple of decent but simple country boys, who were woefully out of their depth in the cut-throat world of High Finance, and a vulnerable street girl. Of course, it would have to be her! It was her moment to show her mettle and dedication to the cause.

Simon nodded, showing consensus among the three of them.

"I will lead the meeting as well as I can and try to buy us some time for when Jez comes back. I just need to take a few minutes of 'me-time' to compose myself."

She went to over to sit the sofa. Holding her core muscles taut and sitting upright, she closed her eyes, and began to perform Buddhist breathing exercises, which she had learned in a student society back at Harvard during her first year.

Although she was not in the habit of practising daily meditation, it was something that she had come to rely on as a safety measure in times of stress.

Counting slowly to herself from one to nine, she breathed in while visualising a huge snake entering her mouth, headfirst, and passing deep into her lungs until it was completely inside her. Then, as she exhaled, she imagined breathing the snake back out into the air, counting backwards down from nine. In this way, she was able to clear her mind of all other thoughts.

"Lavinia, we need to get started," said Simon impatiently.

Lavinia returned to the table refreshed, sat behind her open laptop and started the virtual meeting, which Simon, Andy and Maggie each joined separately from their phones.

She noticed that approximately twenty additional people had joined, some of whom had been present in Ingatestone earlier that year, and a few who still remained in the village. She began to speak.

"Hello everybody. I think you all know me but, just to remind you, I am Lavinia Finkelstein. I have been here in Ingatestone for several months working as part of the New Life movement and helping to set up our corporation. Welcome to you all. It's great to see familiar faces and thank you so much for your sincere support and involvement.

"I'm sure you must be wondering why it's me that is opening the meeting and not Jez. Well, I am sorry to say that he's not here right now and we haven't been able to contact him."

This statement was immediately followed by many anxious gasps and exclamations coming from the attendees.

"Of course, we are all concerned because we have never known him not to show up. But, hopefully, he will be back soon, and we will let you know as soon as we have any news.

"Since Jez isn't here right now, Andy, Simon and Maggie have asked me to lead this meeting. Unfortunately, many of us have been targeted with some unflattering stories about Jez on social media. Now, make no mistake, we have been getting deliberately targeted by people who hate what we stand for. People who make lots and lots of money out of burning down the rainforests, polluting the rivers and seas, and destroying the homes of tribal people and magnificent animals. They are trying to destabilise our organisation by discrediting our leader and halting our momentum.

"I spoke with Jez, yesterday, about some the reports we have seen of his earlier life. Now, he was always honest with us about the fact that he had gone off the rails in the past and done things that he wasn't proud of. We can't get away from that. But the past is the past and I am quite sure that Jez is sincere about wanting to make the world better now. I still believe in him, his integrity and what he stands for. And I hope that you do, too. We are operating on a higher plane now. We have a great opportunity and a platform to change things for the better.

"I personally know for sure that we have been making a positive impact in the world of commerce. Our work has helped to trigger a rush of investment in ethical companies. So please don't quit now. Let's stick together. The stakes are too high for us to fail!"

Suddenly the screen on Lavinia's screen went fuzzy. The meeting had been hijacked. After a few seconds, a scene materialised with three men standing outdoors, in the dark, next to a bonfire. It was dark, and the bonfire only glowed enough to illuminate the immediate vicinity. But Lavinia could clearly see that two of the men were wearing black clothing and pig masks. Between them stood the other man, with his hands pulled behind his back and a hood over his head. On the ground in front of them, there lay an open casket.

The meeting was still running, and horrified shrieks were heard from around the world. The New Life members sensed that something truly awful was about to happen. Then the smaller of the masked men spoke – his voice was electronically cloaked.

"Hello, you bunch of hippies. We are old friends of your mate, Jez. We've got a nice surprise for you. It's the man you've all been waiting for. And here he is." He tore off the hood to reveal Jez's gagged face. Then he removed the gag, held a pistol up to his temple and shouted, "Come on let's hear you squeal!"

Both masked men let out electronically distorted, metallic laughs, accompanied by some desperate cries from the audience.

"We knew you wouldn't want to miss the star attraction. But it's getting late and it's time for little Jezzy boy to go to sleep. We are going to make him comfortable for the night. Let's put him in his bed, shall we?"

They pushed Jez down into the casket. He offered little resistance as they closed the lid. Then they carried the casket backwards and lowered it into a freshly dug hole in the ground. "Sleep well, little Lamb!"

The tall man picked up a shovel and began to scoop earth over the top of the casket.

Suddenly Lavinia's screen went blank.

"Quick!" she cried, urgently. "Si, Andy, come with me. We've got to rescue Jez. I've got some friends that can help us to track him down.

"Let's get the Land Rover. You drive, Andy! There's no time to lose. Maggie, you stay here and keep an eye on things. Don't worry, we'll look after him."

Andy grabbed the keys for the Land Rover from a hook by the door and rushed outside. Lavina and Simon followed quickly behind him, turning to smile and blow a kiss to a distraught Maggie as they left.

They piled into the vehicle. Lavinia took the passenger seat, already on the phone to her cyber security contacts.

"Where to?" asked Andy.

"They've tracked down the location of Jez's mobile to the A414 close to Ongar. It looks like he was there around an hour ago. There's no time to lose!" she replied.

They approached the farm gates. Simon jumped out to fling them open and then they screeched off down Hall Lane to begin their desperate mission to save Jez.

Chapter 13

Jez lay in darkness and listened to the soft thudding sound of the soil being shovelled systematically on top of the casket. It was a surprisingly relaxing sound, considering the dire circumstances, almost like raindrops falling on a roof. He was also aware of some muffled voices which sounded surprisingly vulnerable, considering who their owners were.

Jez knew very well that he was in mortal danger, yet he was still holding out hope that he would somehow be saved. Nothing was impossible for a man of faith! He resisted the urge to cry out or to try to kick his way out of the coffin. He knew that was futile. Surely his God would protect him and show him the correct next course of action at the right moment.

And if these were to be the final moments of life, then he must live them with dignity, love and forgiveness.

To silence the inner voice of panic, he began to think about his dearest friends. A tear ran from the corner of his eye and into his ear as he realised that he might not see them again.

His thoughts first turned to John. Still in an induced coma after three months, his body had been slowly repairing itself and doctors were optimistic that he would eventually recover. This was a man who had taught him by example and had shown him how to put others before himself.

It was almost miraculous that John had made it this far. He had also been ravaged by drink in his youth, and had ended up living under a polythene sheet in a forest near Hertford for several years. His only companions there had been his small dog, Jack, and his bottle of sherry.

John had been born with a hair lip and cleft palette, which his mother had been unable to cope with. She had been incapable of showing him love. Quite irrationally, she had felt that it was all his fault and that he was punishing her and showing her up in public. And then she died of cancer when he was fifteen.

Although the deformity had been later corrected by surgery, he had worn his feelings of injustice and rejection on the outside. Every time that somebody looked at him the wrong way it had seemed as if they were either repulsed by his ugliness or overwhelmed with pity. And these feelings had got him into plenty of trouble.

Many years ago, he had suffered a massive heart attack in the centre of Hertford. An ambulance was called to take him to hospital, but he had refused to go without Jack. Fortunately, a kindly old lady, who witnessed the heart attack, agreed to look after the little dog until John got back. Then he had experienced no less than eleven more heart attacks in the next 48 hours. Amazingly, he pulled through. He just did not seem to be able to die!

During the last of this sequence of heart attacks, John had felt that he had heard God speaking directly to him. The way he liked to tell it was that God had commanded him, "John, Stop beating yourself up and start working for me!"

Anyway, he had not touched alcohol since that day. He had spent his first few weeks of recovery living in a homeless hostel with active drunks and junkies. But, day by day, he had got stronger and he had since dedicated most of his time to helping others. Jez had been his closest friend of all. What a gift to have had the love and friendship of a man such as John!

The thudding noise of the soil being shovelled above him continued. Jez was starting to feel uncomfortably hot. His whole body was sweating profusely, and the air was already becoming stale. He started to think about Simon and Andy. How brash and arrogant they had seemed when he had first seen them getting on the train at Stratford. But that had just been a performance – he had known straight away that they were good boys and that they had the potential to become great men.

Simon did not belong in the City. His heart was too big. He cared too much about others. And he was extremely sensitive: scared of ridicule and humiliation and plagued with feelings of inadequacy.

It had been a real joy to see him express his musical skills to great acclaim and this had really helped with attracting followers to the New Life movement. Simon was a true friend and one that he could always rely on!

Andy was more confident than Simon and more comfortable in his skin. He had been reluctant to join with Jez at first but the fact that he had done so was mainly out of intense loyalty to his best friend. He could certainly walk-the-walk in the banking world if he wanted to. But deep down he was just another good old country boy.

And then there was Lavinia. A wonderful woman, brave and sassy. She treated everyone with respect and she instinctively knew how to put people at their ease.

Of course, she had had a privileged background, quite the opposite of John's. Strong principles came naturally to her – they had not been born out of suffering. He felt sure that she was destined to change the world for the better.

Suddenly he was cast back to his childhood. His father was chiding him for a catalogue of perceived failings, counting them out on his fingers, his every word stabbing at his heart like a dagger. His father had once been the person whom he had most adored in the world but who had never really understood him.

"Dad. I love you. Dad. God bless you, Dad," he whispered.

Now Jez could feel his heart pumping faster and faster, running out of control. His thoughts turned to dear Maggie. She had given him so much love and support. A sweet girl who had suffered terribly but had overcome her problems and turned her life around.

And then he had experienced that beautiful moment of tenderness with her, just once, a tenderness that had been denied to him for so long.

The sounds of the shovelling and the voices were now much quieter. Jez was struggling to breathe, he felt that he was starting to lose consciousness. No – this was not how it was meant to end.

Finally, in desperation, Jez cried out inside the casket, "God, if you really exist then help me! It's not meant to end like this. Don't give up on me!"

∗ ∗ ∗

Lavinia, Simon and Andy listened anxiously to the update from Darryl Lipinski, leading cyber security investigator, also known as 'hacker', as they sped through the winding country lanes towards Ongar.

"We are working to trace the device that intercepted your meeting, Lavinia. It seems that they routed it through the Dark Web, using a virtual private network tunnel, to conceal the source. Don't worry. We've got a backdoor into pretty much every type of router out there on the net. We can sniff out packets and trace them back to exactly where this happened. Our whole team is on it."

"Thanks, Darryl. But what can we do in the meantime? They can't have gone too far from here?"

"Can you guys think of any clues you saw on the screen when they were in your meeting?" he replied.

"There was a bonfire!" Lavinia exclaimed without hesitation.

"That could be a useful clue," continued Darryl. "We can get access to drone data from your vicinity and we can check whether anything might have been spotted. But that's a bit of a long shot."

"They must have done this somewhere private, far away from other people," said Simon. "They wouldn't have wanted to get caught and they must have dug that hole in the ground beforehand."

"Good point, Si," said Andy.

"Hold on. We're getting some intel through," Darryl interrupted. "We are searching for locations where there were abnormal spikes of network activity at the time of the incident. We've got a couple of candidates."

"Go on," said Lavinia.

"Well the first is in Terminus Street, Harlow. Could it be there?"

"I don't think so," said Simon. "That's right in the centre of Town. It's too busy there…quick: what else have you got?"

"Okay," continued Darryl, "another location is just coming through now. North Mymms Park. Do you know that? It looks like it's in the middle of nowhere. Somebody was generating a lot of network traffic there at the time of the incident."

"I've heard of that," responded Andy. "I think it's some kind of Stately Home. That could be it! Let's head over there as fast as possible. Lavinia, get the satnav on your phone set up to take us there. Darryl, you let us know if you get any more info."

There was no time to lose. The Land Rover sped along the A414 in the direction of Hertfordshire.

∗ ∗ ∗

Steve was continuing to shovel soil on top the coffin in which Jez was entombed. His whole body was shaking. He was actually feeling pretty bad about what he was doing to Jez, but he just kept on doing it anyway.

"Hurry up, Steve," snapped Maxie. "We need to get the hell out of here."

81

"Well why don't you give me a hand, instead of shouting at me?" Steve replied.

"How many shovels do you see?"

"Er, just one, actually."

"Exactly! So shut the fuck up and get on with it, you sorry piece of shit!"

All of a sudden, Maxie noticed something strange coming from the nearby barn, like a huge black carpet rolling out towards them. It was accompanied by a ghostly sound of hissing and squeaking.

"What the hell is that?" exclaimed Steve as a huge crowd of rats arrived at their feet. The rats climbed up their trouser legs, and bit into their soft flesh. Maxie screamed as a particularly large and vicious rat bit directly into his groin.

The men managed to detach the rats by jumping and flapping their hands.

"Quick, leg it back to the motor!" shouted Maxie, above the squeaking noise of the rats. Steve dropped his shovel and they sprinted to their car in order to make their getaway. Despite their injuries, they found that they could outrun the animals and make it back to safety without suffering any further attacks.

As soon as they were inside the car, Steve revved the engine and drove away. "That was spooky. I ain't staying around here any longer."

"We must have disturbed a great big colony of the bastards! Anyway, at least we put that shithead under the ground first," replied Maxie, lighting a cigarette and sitting back to relax. "*He* ain't going nowhere!"

* * *

The Land Rover had arrived at the entrance to North Mymms Park and was now travelling along the narrow lane towards the Manor House.

"Please God, let Jez be okay," said Lavinia, clasping her hands together.

As they approached the car park at the end of the lane, Simon spotted the glowing embers of a fire in a field to their left. "This must be it. I can feel it. Let's hope we're not too late."

They all got out of the vehicle and ran into the field. Sure enough, they could see a freshly dug hole in the ground next to the remains of a bonfire, just as they had seen on their screens earlier that evening.

Andy, being the most athletic, was the first to arrive at the scene. He looked down into the hole, and cried out in surprise, "What the hell?"

Lavinia and Simon caught up with him a few seconds later. "Oh my God!" exclaimed Lavinia as she looked down to see the open and empty casket below her. There was no sign of Jez to be seen.

Chapter 14

It was the first Friday in October. A month had passed since the abduction of Jez and there had been no further clue as to his whereabouts. His closest friends were meeting to at his cottage, where Maggie was still living.

Lavinia, Simon and Andy were sitting with her at the kitchen table. There was another familiar figure with them that evening, whom they were all delighted to see.

"It's just great that you are getting back on your feet again and you're out of hospital. We were all so worried about you," said Lavinia.

The old man sitting opposite smiled and his craggy face exploded into a happy mesh of deep lines.

"You shouldn't have worried. I'm pretty much indestructible, you know. It's very sweet of you, Maggie, to let me stay here for a while and recuperate. There's nothing better than to breathe the country air and hang around with my friends."

"Plus there's plenty of work for you to do around the farm, as soon as you feel strong enough, John," teased Maggie with a gentle chuckle. She had made some ad hoc rearrangements to the cottage to create private sleeping space for each of them, insistent that John have use of the permanent bed, despite his protestations.

Since they both loved Jez most of all, it was comforting for them to be spending time together while they awaited news of their friend.

"Don't you worry, girl. I am as strong as an ox. I'll be out there ploughing them fields single-handed in no time," he replied.

Everybody laughed.

"So, what are you all up to now?" asked John. "Are you planning to stay here in Essex, Lavinia, or are you going to go back to America?"

"I'm going to stay here this year, and complete my university studies online," Lavinia replied. "I don't feel like I could leave without knowing what's happened to Jez. And you know that I am totally committed to our cause. Before I came here, I was just drifting through life. Everything had been handed to me on a plate and it seemed like I only had to turn up to be successful. Coming over here has been such an adventure. Now I feel that my life has some real purpose. Plus, I have you guys."

"Lavinia," said Simon. "I've been talking it over with Maggie and Andy and we all feel that you ought to be in charge of the Corporation, in Jez's absence. It was your idea and you've done all the work to set it up."

"That's right," said Andy. "You understand business and politics and you know all the right people. Plus, you are a brilliant girl!" He gave her a cheeky wink.

"I'm sure that is what Jez would have wanted, too, Lavinia," said Maggie, smiling. "If, and when, he returns to us, we can talk about it again."

Lavinia was grateful for their support, but it was tempered by the anxiety that they were all suffering regarding their missing leader. "Of course I will, thank you. I know we have to keep the momentum going even though we are all so desperately worried."

"Good girl!" said John. "Um, I'm sorry to ask this, but I don't suppose you've heard anything from the police, have you?"

"I'm afraid not. The men that abducted Jez seem to have done a good job covering their tracks. And my Cyber Intelligence friends have also drawn a blank. But, hey! We must stay positive. No news is good news, right!"

"That's right, girl. We must stay positive indeed! And you boys…are you still working for that dodgy bank?"

"We are, for the moment," replied Simon, "but we both want to leave, don't we, Andy?"

"Yeah, mate," replied Andy.

"I hope that we will be able to create full-time roles for you both in New Life Corporation once we get that off the ground again. Would you like that?" offered Lavinia.

"Oh, that would be great," Simon replied. Andy also nodded enthusiastically.

"You never know, boys, you might be able to do some good work while you are still working in the City. You may find somebody there who really needs your help," suggested John. "Hey Maggie, the smell of your soup, bubbling on the stove is making me hungry. And you know I need to build myself back up. Do you think we could have some, please?"

* * *

After dinner, the friends continued to talk late into the night. They reminisced about all the events they had shared together over the year. They were determined to continue to fulfil the mission of the New Life movement.

"How about a little music?" proposed John. "I heard you've been learning guitar, Andy, mate."

"Oh, I've just learned to strum a few chords. Nothing special."

"Come on, mate. It'll cheer us all up to have a singsong. Is that your guitar in the corner there?"

"Yes, go on, Andy," said Maggie. "Let's do Seek Ye First the Kingdom of God – that was the first video we ever put out. Lavinia, John, do you want to sing along with me?"

Andy fetched the guitar and sat back down at the table. He began to play the chord sequence, and Maggie joined in with singing.

Seek ye first the Kingdom of God
And His righteousness
And all these things shall be added unto you
Hallelujah, Hallelujah.

Then Simon and Andy took over with their rapping.

Simon and Andy, working in the City,
Living the high life, but something was missing.
Drunk guy tried to slash us. The rats was a-hissing.
Met a girl called Maggie. She was homeless and pretty.

Finally, they all sang the chorus together, led, as always, by Maggie's heavenly voice.

Hallelujah, Hallelujah,
Hallelujah, Hallelujah, Hallelujah

Once it was over, they relaxed, and sat in silence for a while, enjoying the moment, until, suddenly, they heard footsteps outside the front door.

"Did you hear something? I'll go over and check it out," said Simon. He walked over and opened the door cautiously. Standing in the dark was a rough looking man with, sunken cheeks and an unkempt beard. He was wearing a hoodie and tracksuit trousers.

"Can I help you, Sir?" said Simon.

"Simon, don't you recognise me? It's me, Jez!" replied the man.

"Oh God! Of course, it is." Simon rushed forward and gave Jez a hug. Then he stepped back from the doorway. "Come in, Jez, come in!"

Jez entered the cottage and Andy and Lavinia rushed over to also to hug the frail and dishevelled figure.

"Jez. It's so good to see you," gasped Lavinia.

Maggie and John remained sitting at the table. John because his movements were still restricted due to the state of his health and Maggie because she was simply too emotionally overwhelmed at that moment to be capable of standing.

Jez walked over to the table and offered them both a hand to hold. "Maggie, John, my beloved friends. It's so good to see you. I'm sorry that I haven't been in touch."

Everyone was relieved that Jez had returned to them but, at the same time, disturbed by his diminished outward state. They had lots of unanswered questions. Where had he been? Why was he so thin? And how on earth had he escaped from being buried alive in a coffin? He stepped back from the table and addressed the group, his voice trembling.

"Listen to me a moment, please, all of you. I'm sorry but I can't stay long because I don't want to put any of you in danger. I have to move on, but I really needed to see you one last time before I go.

"Don't worry about me. I will be fine. I will always hold you in my heart. You are my closest and truest friends. I love each one of you very much."

His turned his eyes to everybody in turn and finally to Maggie, where they rested the longest. "Very much indeed.

"I know that you will support each other, and I hope that you will carry on with our work. The world needs people like you."

Everybody knew intuitively what this meant. There was no point in saying any more. Jez had always been straight with them. This would be the last time that any of them would see him. Simon began to sob, and Lavinia put her arm around him.

Jez walked back to the front door and pulled it open. He turned around, smiled and blew a kiss to his five friends, then turned back towards the open door and was gone in an instant. Simon rushed outside, calling "Jez, Jez, come back!" Lavinia and Andy hurried after him. But when they arrived outside there was no sign of Jez at all. He seemed to have vanished into the evening mist.

Lavinia and Andy rushed over to Simon, who was weeping uncontrollably, and comforted him. John had managed to walk over to the front door to check that they were all right. He remained standing in the doorway, smiling kindly towards them.

Maggie remained sitting at the table. She was used to men leaving her, so it came as no great surprise that another one had departed. But this one seemed different from the others.

She placed her hand over her belly to comfort the new life that was growing inside her.

Printed in Great Britain
by Amazon